THE BOSS IS DEAD

for Leslie

ISBN 1-58510-177-X

Copyright © 2005 Ron Pullins

This book is published by Focus Publishing, R. Pullins & Company, Inc., PO Box 369, Newburyport MA 01950. All rights are reserved. No part of this publication may be reproduced, stored in a retrieval system, produced on stage or otherwise performed, transmitted by any means, electronic, mechanical, by photocopying, recording, or by any other media without the prior written permission of the publisher.

10 9 8 7 6 5 4

The Boss Is Dead

Ron Pullins

Focus Publishing

Early Morning

- I -

The bears stand motionless on the roof waiting for the boss. The bears do not move in the morning. Mary Lee approaches in her brown Dutch boy hat. She walks the shoulder of High Hawk Road. By Ludi's Big Town Mall, past the gas station, the strip mall, a bagel shop. A red Saab is parked out front. The driver eats a bagel and cream cheese squeezes out the edge. The Lucky Plate serves breakfast.

Mary Lee stops. Looks up. The bears stand on the flat brown roof, square like a paper hat. Twelve purple Burger Bears waiting for the day to begin.

I don't like this, Mary Lee says. I don't like this at all.

She breathes deep and heads up the drive. Her stride is determined. She is small. Her cheeks show age, slight rouge on white skin, skin drawn back tight over her cheeks like a thin sheet pulled over the face of a dead woman. Her hair is long, and straight, and black with a violet shine. It hangs loose to her shoulders. Mary Lee has worked at Interburger since the beginning. The store here on High Hawk Road is the original. These were the first bears. There are many other stores now. The founder has died, his predecessor retired, Keith is the boss at High Hawk Road. Mary Lee is the last of the original crew.

She has always been the Front Line Manager. She has been offered other jobs. But she stays here at High Hawk Road, Front Line Manager, earning what she needs, doing what she knows. She will never be fired. She is as fixed and as eternal as the grease barrels out back. As the bears on the roof.

Keith's car is here.

That's not right, she says.

Keith's never here this early. Something's wrong.

Keith is the boss, and Mary Lee will always have a boss. She will always report to someone, although she knows her duty better than anyone else. It is as if what she chooses is the proper way. No rules guide her. She works with a natural grace. She cannot work harder or move faster than she already does on her own. She cannot be without a boss and yet no boss can tell her what to do better than she already does. She wants to do her work and be left alone. She is a mystery.

She walks up the drive and to the rear of the store. Keith's van is parked under a cottonwood tree. It is lavender with pin stripes along both sides and swirls on the doors. A large orange sun is painted on each side, and across this bright orange sun stretches the dark silhouette of a deer with antlers. The small windows on each side in the back bulge out like eyes on a fly.

Where's Keith? she asks.

This van shouldn't be here. Mary Lee taps on the dark glass window. She tries the door and it is locked.

I don't like this, she says. I don't like this at all.

Rats rustle in the dumpsters, running free through the trash. Garbage bags are piled high, like a green dome. Flies come and go from the grease barrels. Mary Lee turns the key to the store, the handle gives way and she opens the back door.

It is cool inside. There is a hum of refrigeration. Air rolls out and smells heavy, rotten, wrong.

Keith? Mary Lee asks.

It is too quiet. Maybe the night crew has left meat out to spoil. Or, maybe someone forgot to clean the shake machine and the mix has gone sour. She takes a cautious heavy step inside, her tennis shoe firm on the floor, but she withholds her weight and all commitment. The bright summer morning behind her makes the inside darker still, shadows of the store, the presence of Burger Bear.

Keith, she asks again. Are you here?

At that moment the flies swarm up. Hundreds of them. Thousands of them. Fat and thick and slow. Like customers on a busy Friday noon, indifferent, impatient, demanding. Stupid customers, big and fat and knocking about between things in lazy flight, not caring. Off the walls, and up and off the cool steel sink, off the ceiling where they have been hanging, sleeping, waiting for time to begin. Up from the red tile floor, swarming around the back line, brushing by Mary Lee, indifferent whether they hit a living thing or stone. Then escape outside and into the morning.

Lordie, Mary Lee says, waving her hands in front of her face. Keith?

The remaining flies hover like tiny airborne machines, bumping here and there, landing, resting. Mary Lee walks carefully, they are a carpet on the tiles.

Are you there? Is anyone there?

Then there is Keith, slumped over the grill, his face, his neck, his right arm, and his shoulder, slow cooked like thick steak, hard as an old hamburger, his eyes popped out like eggs and fried on the grill. His left arm has slipped into the grease and been French fried to the bone. Maggots are swimming in the soup of his brain.

The boss is dead. The mountains ring out.

Keith! Mary Lee cries out. Get up.

She shakes him, but the boss is stuck to the grill. She brushes away the flies, picks up the phone and dials.

Chris, she says. Chris, she repeats. Get up, Chris. Wake up. We need you, Chris. You must come in.

-2-

The phone is ringing far away. I am sleeping, dreaming. I pull the receiver in under the sheets.

"Chris," Mary Lee says again. "Say something. I've got other things to do."

"The boss is dead," I whisper. I have never felt such joy.

"Mary Lee," she says again. Her voice is tiny, tinny, far away. "Get up, Chris, and get your butt in gear. It's after nine. You are supposed to be here in fifteen minutes. It's Burger Bear day—it's Burger Bust! Keith expects you to help out on the back line."

"Burger Bust?" I repeat in a whisper. "Today? Where's Beth?" Except for me—and I am sitting up now—the bed is empty, cold. All that remains of Beth is a depression in the mattress. My throat is dry, my eyes full of sleep. I hardly hear myself speak. I am hardly speaking. I wonder if Mary Lee hears me.

"Did you forget?" Mary Lee says. "Burger Bear today. Burger Bust. Get it together quick, buddy. Keith is going to set records."

Keith and his records. I am night manager six nights a week, and he has been working me days now as well—whenever he needs extra help. I am salaried and thus cheap help. Everyone but Keith and I is on the clock. The more hours I work, the cheaper I am.

"I'm hanging up now," Mary Lee squawks. "I'm hanging up. Are you awake? Are you coming in? We open at eleven. We need your help. Answer me, Chris."

Isn't he dead, I think. Caesar ist morte.

"Answer me, Chris?" Mary Lee says. "I have to go. Keith wants to know. Are you coming in?"

"The boss is dead ," I say. "Isn't he now a burger for bugs?" I giggle.

"Half an hour," she says.

"Tell Keith the flies are delighted with his eyes."

"The flies are what?" Keith says. He takes the phone. "Get your butt out of bed, Chris. It's Burger Bust. We have no time for your fooling around."

Sweet Keith. Dear Keith. Keith on the phone. Keith alive. Keith the Boss. Keith doesn't wait, but hangs up. So I have been dreaming, and now I am awake.

-3-

Beth is gone. Tall, skinny, her skin as white as fine paper, smooth as marble, dim freckles on her face and—now I know, after last night, after looking at her, studying her, like some explorer of all the terrain of her lovely self—a stream of muted freckles flows down her shoulders, down her back, along the front of her thighs, flowing as subtle and harmless as stones in a mountain stream, the loving color of rust on a new nail, all the way to her toes, and off her toes, red on her nails, and, like a stream that has reached a shelf of red rock , it falls over and down and away. Her knees are thin and long, betraying only the slightest curve. Her neck stretches like that of a crane, and she felt fragile under me in the dark, the bones of a bird fluttering in my hand. I had been afraid I would damage her. I lifted her up and on me, to protect her, as we made love.

I live alone in a studio apartment near midtown. I live in a no-bedroom apartment, a studio. A cold, creaky Murphy bed pulls down from the wall. The first night I rented this place two years ago I pulled the bed down and I have not put it up since. Someone left an old oak rocker when they moved out. It is my best piece of furniture. My clothes hang across the rocker's back, shirts three deep on one side, pants folded across the back, a tie grease-spattered from days and nights working at Interburger, Inc. I have made a table from boxes of books. From time to time I dig through this mess for something to read. I am partial to poetry. When I eat at home, I eat on the table, and I read poetry.

I wake slowly. My undershorts are hanging from the rabbit ears antenna of my television. Now, I remember, I have slept with Beth, who is assistant manager at one of the shopping mall stores. She came home with me, we made love, then she got up early and left. I do not know why—after all these months—I was successful last night, but I don't care. Her scent lingers in the sheets, her heat, the tone in her throat. She has left her shape depressed in the mattress and pillows. Her sweet, slow moving energy lingers in my small room. I think, love is confusion, and I am in love.

It is morning. My ceiling fan turns slow. I fell for Beth the first time I saw her. We met as trainees at the Interburger commissary. She had been promoted from a counter girl, and I had just been hired. We were in the patty section. Interburger ships meat into the commissary, grinds it into hamburger, then shapes it into patties according to strict specifications—so it fries just so, and tastes just right, and fits exactly on the bun and no more, so it requires a precise amount of relish, two slices of pickle and twelve bits of chopped onion. One shake of salt from special shakers made so one shake is the precise requirement. No more.

"You're very young," I said to Beth. Very young, I meant, to be a manager. She did not know me. A piston came down—a fist of steel—on a ball of meat, spreading it evenly into a round patty, then again and again, patty, patty, as a mechanical arm with its spatulated hand scooped up patties and stacked them on wax paper. Meat, paper, meat, paper, in precise round towers of burgers-to-be.

Beth turned to me and smiled. "You're not so old I couldn't catch you. But first I'd have to want to."

Beth had worked at Interburger as a counter girl in high school, then continued at another store while she worked her way through college. She was lovely, a looker, though in no way glamorous—wiry, thin, strong willed, and bright. Men who loved big busts were disappointed in Beth, but not I. I like her boyish charm. I like it, too, that she laughed a lot, and that she laughed at things I said, and did so even that first day. She laughed at her own quick reply to me, then turned away, to study how properly to process meat into patties with a giant steel fist.

"Coulda only've been invented by a man," she said, and all the men around her laughed. Men always cluster around her, but at that moment she looked back at me and smiled. Humor has that bond, and she knew I understood. She made me want to make her laugh, then and always after.

Beth knew everyone at Interburger. She has a comfortable way with other people, and of getting to know them. She knew all the managers and they watched out for her. I heard her laughter above the frying of meat at the learning grill, above the fans and above the monotonous drawl of Richard Baptist, legendary grillman who owned a large share of Interburger, Inc. He was in charge of marketing and training. He flipped hamburgers like no other grillman—fast, accurate, unflappably, cutting hamburgers off the grill with his spat in one swoop, leaving the grill as clean as when it was first fired up, then flipping the patties around so they land in neat rows to fry on their other sides.

"The spat must be sharp," he said to the trainees. "As sharp as a razor, as straight as a knife." He sharpened the front of his spat by running it along a file. "Flat, so it doesn't gouge the grill. To gouge the grill, that is a sin. Keep the grill clean all day, no build up. Then meat can cook. These are the signs of a great grillman." Then Baptist looked up, a madness in his eyes. He slapped the frying meat with the flat of his spat. "We are not bakers, but fry cooks. And meat only fries right on shining clean metal."

From that moment on I had resolved to know Beth. I had dreamed about her. She and the thought of her sustained me during my many long months at Interburger.

Beth has landed a job in a mall. She has always been lucky in that respect. The men in the management of Interburger, Inc. liked her and looked out for her. The mall stores are the choice assignments. The mall stores are not open late, and they have assistant managers instead of night managers. Free standing stores like High Hawk Road are open until midnight. Some say the future is in the mall. Others think we can grow only if we are unencumbered by the rules of the mall. Whatever is best, we trainees have no choice in the matter. We take the jobs offered us, and we keep in touch with each other.

I have kept in touch with Beth. Keith leaves the store around five, after which the Interburger on High Hawk Road is mine to manage. I manage the dinner rush, which is half the size of lunch or less. Around nine I start my crew on clean up—mopping the floors, wiping down the tables, picking up the parking lot, washing windows, polishing and restocking the front line, the back line, the grill, taking out the trash, cleaning the fryers, scrubbing the grease filters, washing and disassembling the shake machine, and taking out the grease. After months of talking on the phone, Beth finally came over one night to visit and helped me close the store on High Hawk Road.

Closing is a crazy time. I make it so. Craziness saves on labor. Night business being what it is, even a minimal crew is expensive. Once we close, I get the store cleaned quickly and get the crew off the clock. It is easy to move a young crew. If they hate the work, they finish it quicker, even though they need the money ineptitude might earn them.

"Could I turn off half the grill, Mr. Mann?" Bryan asks about nine.

I let him turn off half the grill and ice it down.

"Mr. Mann?" the girls out front ask as soon as Bryan starts icing down the grill. "Can we break down the shake machine? There ain't no one coming in and it's gonna rain."

"Can't break down the shake machine, girls," I say. "We have to wait for closing. But one of you can mop up front, half the lobby and when that's dry, the other half." Or whoever is the newest on the crew, or someone who needs a little discipline, maybe someone I think is stealing on the side, I assign them the toilets to clean. If they complain, I say, "If not you, then who?" That has no answer, unless there is someone even newer on the crew, or someone they don't like, or someone they think is not doing his or her share, someone they think might be stealing from them. I follow up with, "Just do it and I don't care how long it takes as long as it's clean enough for Keith to take a shit."

They laugh, and I laugh, though most of them do not hate Keith as much as I do. Even so, we all agree Keith's idea of clean has come from his ridiculous army training. He worked with dogs in Korea, and we figure he is fastidious because he had to sponge so many butts on so many dogs. Keith does things just so and he expects us to do the same.

Still I get them to move quick and clean up. They glower if some late night customer comes in and wants to use the toilet, or wants fries, or a milk shake, anything that will make a mess on what has already been cleaned. On a good night High Hawk Road is cleaned twenty minutes after the doors are locked and I have turned off the bears. My goal has been to get it down to fifteen minutes.

The bears. When the store is closed, the bears must die. When the night manager leaves, the bears must be silent. At closing I shut off the outside lights and the power to the bears. I let my crew go, lock the doors and relax in the office to count the money. Beth has been helping for a month or so. Sometimes she stays even later and we talk. We sit in the office or outside in my car listening to jazz on the radio. Lately we sometimes go out for a bite to eat at the late night restaurant that caters to after hours people who work in bars and restaurants. A few times we have even gone to Box-a-Burger where kids from restaurants all around the suburbs gather after work on late summer nights.

Box-a-Burger has become our greatest rival. It sits a half mile up High Hawk Road. It is not much of a place, a little drive-through restaurant that serves hamburgers, cheeseburgers, fries, Cokes, and coffee, but their food is high quality, and comes quick, and is only served through a single drive-by window. According to Keith, it is unnatural and unhealthy for people to drive and eat. Box-a-Burger is not a restaurant at all, he says, but sacrilege, a food cart missing its wheels. It won't last, he says. It can't, he says, because he fired Dandison, the worthless ass who now manages that store — our greatest competition. Dandison had my job before me. Now Dandison takes delight in stealing our customers.

Sometimes customers come into our store and order the "Big Box with Cheese." That enrages Keith. Even if we are busy he takes off his apron and runs out front and explains in heated detail the difference between the horrible abomination called the Big Box and our own fine crafted BurgerRoo. The little cart without wheels gets to him. He hates Dandison.

Frequently now that it is summer my night crew joins others behind the Box-a-Burger after work. It is an odd, but comforting place in the dark, in the quiet of a city when the traffic dies away, especially on warm nights. They are hard working kids who gather there. They have enough money for a beer or two, or wine, or a cigarette or two, or pot, and they like to sit in their cars in the dark – and they all have cars and love them – and talk and hang out. They are good kids, for the most part, and work hard and pay taxes.

I like them best then, out of the store, off the clock, in the dark. I had brought Beth along several times. They thought it was novel, their boss coming to their place. They even let me play jazz on my car radio. My favorite station starts the evening mellow—standard jazz, even rather trite jazz. But as it grows late, the jazz takes more risks, and that was the jazz the kids liked most. For a moment it is almost like rock. Then it veers away into numbers and patterns.

Did I say that sometimes I bought beer for the kids? Or wine. In that way I have come to be trusted. I look younger, too, than I am, by ten years or so. They share what they smoke. I share what I buy. Beth is fascinated, and curious about all of it. But she never stays long. I could stay here forever. I have no idea how long the kids stay. As late as I stay, I always leave early.

Dandison manages the Box-a-Burger. It is a tiny store with space inside for no more than four people at one time. The line of cars driving through dwarfs that little box of a place. Because it is so small, and because Dandison owns a share of it, he works all day and all evening seven days a week. Dandison likes to drink. It was a taste he acquired as night manager at Interburger. Now, with nowhere else to go after his work is done at Box-a-Burger, Dandison drinks with the young people. He buys his kids liquor when they ask. He is a friend to his crew, he pays them well, and sometimes it is a struggle to keep my crew from hiring on with him.

At closing, Dandison checks out his place, makes sure it is clean, makes sure it is ready for business in the morning, then he gives a nod and says, "Hey, you little shits, who's ready to go out back and have a drink?" He holds up his six pack of beer and clocks everyone out. Like Jesus with his wine, of course, a dozen kids can share one six pack, and beer remains for all who want it. The kids like Dandison. He is a straight and simple boss.

Dandison's drink of choice is vodka. After an hour or so of drinking with the kids, he wanders back into his Box-a-Burger, locks the door and falls asleep on the floor. That is his way of closing. In the morning, he is the first to work, ready to open the store for another day. Sometimes he goes home and showers and puts on a clean shirt, but not always.

So it has been going this summer—pleasant, and promising, and life is not bad.

Beth came by last night to help me close, but things turned out different. Beth was different. She acted listless, pitching in to help, but dreamy, her mind somewhere else. She looked different, too, that past month. Things she said were not as funny as usual. She laughed at whatever I said, even things that were not funny, and she smiled a lot, often standing so close to me I felt her warmth. Her jeans were tighter, I thought. Even her thin legs had shape, as they came to that place where they curved up around her hips. She smelled different, too, and I sensed her above the grease of that day's frying. When she was there to help us close, she smelled like she had just taken a shower, but more than that.

We cleaned up the store in record time. I clocked the counter girls out, and iced down the grill myself. I even promised them a six pack if they got done in twenty minutes. Tall, gawky Bryan moved like a madman. He ran when he carried the bucket of grease out back to the barrels. He mopped the red tile floor in a frenzy. I made him do it twice, and still he was done quicker than ever before. The girls up front finished in eighteen minutes flat. Whack, whack, whack, whack, they all clocked out and I rewarded them with the beer I had stashed in the cooler. Bryan drove them all to Box-a-Burger, and Beth and I found ourselves alone in the store.

"Wow, alone," I said to her, almost like a joke.

Beth smiled. She was standing close to me, and she did not move, neither stepping towards me nor away. I waited to think of something else to say, but nothing came to mind. Then I realized she was waiting for me. I realized she was not going to resist. It would appear to be my advance, my initiative, but it had been her doing, and I didn't care.

She was lovely. She wore tight jeans and an oversized man's shirt that hung below her hips, its sleeves rolled up just enough to keep her hands free. Loose, alluring, manly, and very sexy.

I did not rush into this. I was afraid of hurting her, or making some mistake. I was uncertain, too, what she wanted. She is very young. I reached over and took her hand which she gave without resistance. It was dark in the back of the store, except for the dim glow of the red exit lights. The machines were off, except for the refrigeration which hummed softly. I heard her breathing. I kissed her hand. She granted me all I asked.

She wore the scent of the oceans. Light filtered through the front of the store, through the window above the now cool steam table, and highlighted the seams of her loose shirt, the shadows the flesh which showed through her shirt.

I was drifting. Neither of us rushed. I put my hand around the small of Beth's back and felt the seam of her shirt and the straps beneath, like a welt against her spine. I pulled her close and we kissed. At first I merely kissed her cheek, but she turned her lips to me and I found her in the dark. She did not resist. I loved it that she was tall, that her lips were next to mine, that her craning neck was easily accessible. Her small breasts pressed against me. I loved her small breasts, feminine but not intrusive, little to keep us apart, yet a barometer of her passion. Beneath her shirt, they ached like I ached. She kissed back, her lips responding to mine. I kissed her forehead, then her hair, and she was buried in me, and by me, wrapped in my arms, and I pressed her to me like she was a part of me. I felt good, and loved, and I wanted to cry, but I held back, wanting to explore further, to see where this would end, or even if it ever would. We kissed again and again, and I felt my back bend, and my knees grow weak. I was dizzy. The room was dark. The floor was not apparent. I was sometimes uncertain where I was, what was level, my eyes half closed. I wanted to lay with her, even here on the red tile floor. I wanted to respond to her yielding by invading. I wanted to fall to the floor like a feather and bring her with me.

"Shouldn't we be going?" she asked.

"Going?"

"The store is closed. Shouldn't we go? Won't they miss us?"

"Oh," I say. "They might. We promised. And they shouldn't know, you know, about us, you know. Company rules."

"Oh, yes."

I did not know what was right to do. I did not want to leave. I had no idea of what was company policy, and had I known I would not have cared. I did not want to let her go or to let this moment escape. The kids would not miss us. I wanted to let my knees give way and slouch to the floor, holding her. I wanted to lay on the cold tiles with her, and find her, explore her at her very center. But I did not want to anger her. She let us slip apart.

I breathed deep, then slowly returned to my duties, walking around the store with her to check that everything was as it should be, that the shades were up, that the doors were locked, that the grill and fryers were turned off, and finally to turn off the bears. We walked across the back line. I held her hand. She followed without resistance like a tow in calm water. I checked that the refrigerator door was shut, the safe was locked, the alarm set. I felt her beside me, and, when I stopped and turned, she was there. Had she given me the slightest cue, I would have stopped all else and embraced her again, but she did not. I held her and pulled her close and gently kissed her lips. She did not refuse. She seemed to melt, but pulled away.

"And are we going to see your friend Ed?" she says.

"Ed?"

"I need some air."

"I see," I said, not really thinking at all, but happily being swept along with feeling. "Me, too," I said. "I'm sorry."

"Sorry?" Beth said.

"Oh, yes," I said, embarrassed and apologetic. "For going so far." It was not that I was sorry, not at all, but that I thought she thought I should be.

"Oh, that," she said. "I don't mind. I enjoyed that. I just don't want to end up making love in a fast food joint. And the kids.... A crew talks."

I laughed. "Oh, yeah," I said. "I agree." But I was lying. I would have made love there, on those red tiles, or anywhere. The kids could talk.

We drove to Box-a-Burger and stayed a while. The kids seemed different that night, and I thought they must know something was different with me. I felt myself wiping my lips as if they saw the lipstick I had tasted. I was careful not to be too deferential to Beth, too courteous, too kind, since that might reveal my passion. That was difficult, even in the shadows behind the Box-a-Burger. I felt queasy, and my voice shook sometimes when I talked. I was not nervous because of the kids, but because of Beth. We leaned against my car in the dark, and listened to the kids and the music, sipped beer. It felt crowded behind the Box-a-Burger, and late.

"Are you hungry?" I asked. "You want to go somewhere?"

"In a while," she said. "I like it here."

"I do, too," I said, but that was a lie. I wanted to take her home. I wanted to go then. I had another beer.

I laughed a little too loud when she said something funny. I laughed when she said anything. I laughed sometimes at the wrong places. The third or fourth time I asked if she was ready to go, she said yes. She drove me back to Interburger where I got my car.

"Well," I said. She was in her car next to mine. "Why don't you follow me home, come in for a while?" It was a crazy thing to say, perhaps the wrong thing, but I did not know how else to span the chasm to my desire.

"Sure," she said, brief and to the point and without pause.

I felt like the dog that had caught the car it had been chasing. I wanted to sing. But I was unsure of what to do now. Everything suddenly seemed perfect and possible.

"It's not much," I said. "My place."

"I don't need much," she said.

"Then follow me."

I had not given a moment's thought to Galinda, but for a change, my car gave me no problems. She started up without hesitation the moment I turned the key. The blue smoke that always accompanied her first waking moments were not seen in the dark. Even her brakes worked, as they sometimes failed to do for unspecified periods of time. Galinda ran that night as smooth as silk. The traffic was light. I rarely tapped Galinda's brakes, and when I did they held. I timed things right and coasted through the lights. I assumed Galinda herself sensed the possibilities. She carried me home without error or hesitation. Beth followed in her car as if we were already deep in dream.

-4-

Morning has come. Despite my inclination, I am unable to stay in bed for long. Beth is gone. I have the sheets pulled up over my head.

I hate Keith. I hate him especially now because he is not dead.

However much I think about sleep, I am awake for the day. I lie there for a while, then summon enough energy to drop my legs over the edge of the bed. I sit up. I lie back down. I sit up. Soon I am on my feet.

Outside, beyond the Venetian blinds, the boulevard sweeps through this old part of the city. When it is dark, the street light falls through the Venetian blinds in stripes across my bed and gives my little studio a formal elegance, appropriate to my recent hours with Beth.

When I had brought her to my apartment, she had sat on the edge of the bed. I had sat down beside her. I turned on the television, as I always do when I come home. It is the light by which I sleep.

"I want to see you," Beth said. I knew what she meant. Without a word, she undressed me, pulling off my pants and socks. She stripped me of underwear, tossing my shorts so they land on the rabbit ears of my TV set. They hung there all night like a ghost. We lay back together. Seeing me, she said, "You look delicious."

Then I undressed her, beginning with the buttons on the front of her shirt.

"Slow," she whispered.

I was nervous and impatient. The gray light of the television outlined us in silver. I no longer remembered having turned it on. We leaned back together, embraced, then fell on the bed. She laughed and turned down the sound with her toe. I switched on my radio which played old jazz all night.

I started to say I loved her, but she stopped me. Patterns in the jazz were saying what I meant. I buried my face in her embrace.

Later, after great pleasure, I fell back and stared up at the ceiling. This little room has a ceiling fan that revolves around a light, but neither works. She laid her arm over me, then pulled herself closer. I held her close, so I didn't have to talk. She rolled about until she seemed curled up in me, warm and damp. Her skin accepted my skin and they merged.

"What do you think?" she asked. Her lips were close to my ear, her hair across my face.

"Nothing," I said.

"Are you happy?" she asked.

"With what?"

"With anything."

"With you."

She laughed lightly.

"And you?" I asked.

"You're a good lover."

"Night manager," I said.

"A good lover," she said, as if correcting me. "You shouldn't confuse the two."

"I mean manager of the night." I laughed.

"Well, I don't know," she says. "A good lover," as if that was exactly what she meant and nothing more.

I had lain there for several hours, spent but with the rush of sex still lingering in my thighs and draping itself across my brain. I could not sleep, but I did not want to think or move, and where she was touching me—her thigh draped across my thigh, my arm around her and under her and drawing her to me, to encourage her to curl up against me, her breasts against my side—our flesh was damp as if fused.

She snored lightly. The radio was playing the right songs, the old ones, ones I had heard years ago, ones that reminded me of my early loves, of driving home after a date alone and blue, of a dozen times my heart had been broken. I remembered those times—the car, the place, the time of day, just where I'd been when I had heard those songs, exactly what it was and who had left me heartbroken, or yearning, or afraid, my youth defined in songs.

The radio played through the night. There were many songs, played in perfect order to make a kind of night sense, an argument for never growing old. I watched the ceiling and heard Beth's snoring. The old tunes mellowed out as the digits on the clock marched towards morning, soft rock fading into softer rock, into tunes I sometimes barely remembered and their messages more obscure.

At night the streetlights outside were a brilliant orange, and the light from them came through the Venetian blinds and fell across the room, across the bed, across the two of us, leaving us entangled in a cage of shadows, bars of light. They faded as day emerged.

I drifted in and out of sleep. At such a time one state is not much different from another. I woke up several times that night, felt her there, then fell back to sleep and into dreams. Sometimes the dreams were of her, sometimes of us together again, and other times dreams of work, or war. Beth—tall, thin and almost innocent—got up sometime after five in the morning, showered, and dressed. I pretended to be asleep as I watched her naked, her lovely small breasts, her long legs, watched as she brushed her teeth, paste on her finger. I heard the door click shut as she left. I heard her car door shut, her car start and then she drove away.

-5-

My car is named Galinda. I have had a car since I was fourteen. I have owned Galinda now two years. It is the worst car I have ever owned. After my divorce, I needed a car quick. It turned out the father of a girl who worked nights was selling the family car and I bought it.

Galinda is a Ford Galaxy. She is my big baby blue Ford, an enormous and empty car, as full of space as her name implies. But she is an old man's car, built in an era of big, cheap American cars, designed to fall apart after 50,000 miles. She was dutifully falling apart when I got her. The brakes are going bad, smoke comes from the exhaust, the power steering no longer works, two tires are misaligned and worn on the shoulders, and water leaks from somewhere under the dash so that the floorboard under the driver's seat is rusting through. The radio, however, is excellent, so much so it was the reason I bought her in the first place. Plus, I needed a car, and she is mostly good, and for two years now she has gotten me where I have needed to go, no problem.

I have come to love Galinda, as one might love a poor sick dying pup, and she has not yet entirely failed me. This morning Galinda starts with a cough from her six cylinders, emits a cloud of smoke, and a blue haze spreads out over the parking lot behind my apartment. We wend our way through the late morning traffic. Galinda fades in high gear, and sometimes fails under the strain of an upward grade, but she works well enough in second, where I leave her, even though in second she is a bit noisier than other cars on the road. I keep to the outside lanes on the streets, and take a route that has few stop signs or lights. I slide through the traffic lights along the way and keep a safe distance between me and any car ahead, avoiding the need ever to stop.

It is a cool summer morning, and the clean air blows in through my open window. I love driving. There are more ads on the radio in the morning, but good songs, too, about summertime, and work, and dying. It is ten by the time I see the purple bears on the roof on High Hawk Road. I turn left up the small incline, pull around back, then gear down sweet Galinda, so she can coast into our regular spot. She bumps the curb and I pull the emergency brake to hold her in place. I have made it again for another day, hooray!

The store is not yet open, and it is quiet out back. Keith's van is there, the reddish sun and deer head painted on its side. He parks a few steps from the rear door. Next to his van is the orange Burger Bear Express, the company bus. Lines of dancing bears are painted on both sides —happy, smiling, dancing, purple bears with hats and ties and canes, and a larger portrait of dancing Burger Bear himself. Burger Bear wears his paper hat, cocked jauntily to one side, 'as is our wont,' as the Manual says, one hand in the air to maintain his balance and the other holding that masterpiece of culinary science, the paragon of nutritional engineering, our economic miracle, the BurgerRoo, two slices of cheese, two patties of meat, a secret sauce of mayonnaise and Thousand Island dressing, sixteen pieces of chopped onion, three pickle slices arranged just so, inside the crown of a toasted bun, the entire wobbly construction held together by a cardboard ring and packed in a cardboard box printed to look like Burger Bear's house.

The garbage out back is ripe and flies buzz around, though not nearly as thick as the flies in my dream.

"Chris!" Mary Lee yells from the rear door. "Keith's waiting."

She lets the screen door slam against the jamb.

The song about summer and longing and love ends, and I turn Galinda off. She sighs. Warm air is rising from the asphalt. There is steady traffic on High Hawk Road. I open the door, stand up and hold on.

-6-

Every Friday all summer long Burger Bear drives the company bus from one Interburger store to another. Kids love our big, furry, funny dancing bear. Parents love free coupons. We depend on Burger Bear to bring in the young crowd.

And today is Burger Bear Day at High Hawk Road. Richard Baptist, Interburger's marketing director, is Burger Bear. He dresses in a suit and tie when he drives the bus to the next store, but once he parks in the store lot he disappears into the back to appear half an hour later transubstantiated—Burger Bear, taller than any man, a creature with a furry butt, neutered, but with claws and feet, and wearing his Burger Bear hat just so, cocked to the side of his purple Burger Bear head. Sometimes the very smallest children cry when they first see him, and it is hard to tell if that is from love or fear.

Baptist invented Burger Bear when he was a grillman at the earliest Interburger stores. Baptist had become a legendary grillman, master of the grill and spat who cooked his way through massive lunch hour rushes—three hundred and sixty, seven hundred and twenty, or even a thousand hamburgers single-handed in an hour, cooked, garnished and wrapped all alone when need be. And he smiled all the while, cracked jokes with the counter girls out front, barely raising a sweat on his brow, never splattering the grease, and keeping on the grill the fine shine of new metal.

Baptist kept a cool head in the middle of even the most crushing lunch hours. When it seemed that everyone else was about to go under in the crush of customers, to collapse under the weight of accumulating chaos of buns and meat and garnish, buried under wrapping and special orders and fries—when someone shouted frantically through the steam table window, "Special Order, BurgerRoo, no mayonnaise," Baptist leaned forward and smiled, "One Roo, no poo." For a moment it did not register out front, then it did, and it took another moment for them to believe, but then they laughed, and laughed, and from that moment on the rush was under control, the entropy of the universe reversed and all things rushed back into order. From time to time the girls could not help but laugh again when they remembered, until finally, like every other rush, that one also petered out into the dullness of the afternoon.

Great grillman though Baptist was, he had also had a lucky break. Interburger had overexpanded in its earlier years and was about to go bankrupt when, fortunately, Baptist's grandmother died, and he inherited her sizable estate. The founder himself had come to Baptist one night where he was working the back line and, while the two cooked burgers together, the founder made Baptist an offer. In return for investing his inheritance in the chain, Baptist would own one quarter of Interburger, Inc. His forever. He could be a manager, if he wanted, or director of the commissary, or director of marketing. If they made a go of it, so the founder said, Baptist would double his money or more. "America is in love with the cheeseburger and fries," the founder had said. "We'll make America love the BurgerRoo, too."

They were an excellent team. Baptist was fast and graceful, and the founder knew when the essence of the meat had been reached as it cooked on the grill, how to toast a bun to perfection, when cheese was soft enough and no more. There were never, it was said, better BurgerRoos cooked than the two of them cooked that night.

"I see a purple dancing bear," Baptist had said.

"A what?"

Baptist had had a vision on the spot, the purple dancing bear, the colors brown and orange, the paper hat worn just slightly cocked to the side. Jaunty, he described it.

"I see it, too," the founder repeated. Then he said it again with more enthusiasm. He garnished the BurgerRoos, the best ever produced. Customers had come back for seconds. "I see it clear."

"I want to be it," Baptist said. "Burger Bear. More than just see it, I want to be the bear."

"I see it, yes. I see you being it," the founder said. "The hat, the spat, the colors. The Hamburger Bear."

"Just Burger Bear," Baptist said. "Jaunty. Just so." He tipped his hat, and consummated the new arrangement.

Not two hours after closing they signed the papers, and the founder got his check. Interburger, Inc., was saved and Burger Bear was born.

Others could do the advertising, print the coupons, schedule the ads. Only Richard Baptist could be Burger Bear. He worked on his act, worked on his costume, worked on his dancing, and then went from store to store for the next dozen years, the living, loving Burger Bear incarnate.

Second to being the Bear, Baptist liked beer. But the Burger Bear costume was a cumbersome outfit, big, and full of stuffing, and it hung from his shoulders by two heavy-duty suspenders. When he became Burger Bear, he found it hard to get in and out of the costume in order to pee. So Baptist cut back on beer and turned to whiskey. It worked. He could go all afternoon on a pint of whiskey and never needed to struggle out of his costume. A little whiskey kept Richard Baptist happy, and laughing, and dealing out free coupons, until some parents complained of the whiskey smell. So Baptist at last settled on gin—which was cheaper anyway, and odorless, and looked a lot like water.

When I pull into the lot that morning I see the Burger Bear bus and look for Baptist.

"Hey, Mr. Baptist," I call out, knocking on the windows of his van. I expect him to be in the back, getting into his costume. Instead I find him in the rear sprawled on the floor, a scrawny man, his feet sticking out of the bus and he himself motionless, staring up at the roof. He wears two bear paws on his feet and a pair of white undershorts and an undershirt. I think he is dead.

"Hey, man, what's wrong? Are you okay?" I shake his foot and pull him out so I can lift up his head. His feet bend to the ground, but he remains prone, breathing heavily, staring at the roof of his van. I smell alcohol. I see an empty bottle of gin.

"Hey, Burger Bear," I say. "You got to get up, man. Kids'll be coming and they might see you. You don't want them to see you like this."

I look towards the store for help, but the back door is shut, and there are no rear windows. No one sees me, or him. "They'll be wanting you, Mr. Baptist," I say, trying to sit him up. "You are the greatest," I say to encouragement him. "Burger Bear! Burger Bear! Burg!—Gurrr!—Roo!!" I sing it as best I can. He is heavy and I am unable to stir him.

He opens his eyes as I sling his arm around my neck, then he closes them again and relaxes back in the van. He is not moving, and I am unable to move him. His head is small, looking shrunken as it sticks out of the enormousness of those paws on his feet. His chest is bare as well, looking thin, pale, an ash white, the color of death, frail.

"Chris!" Keith stands at the back door and yells to me. "You're late. Tell Burger Bear to get his butt in here, too."

The screen door slams shut.

'Help me!" I yell to Keith, but too late.

"Let me alone," Burger Bear says. "I'm sick. I'm dying."

"You are not dying."

"I want to die. Help me die."

I try to get Burger Bear to sit. I sling his arm around my neck again and reach around his waist. "Everybody works at High Hawk Road," I say, repeating one of Keith's favorite lines. "No slackers here. You got to get up. Nobody gets so sick that Keith lets you off. If you are sick enough to think you're too sick to work, then you're able to work. That's what Keith says."

"Just let me alone. Shut the fucking doors and let me sleep. Leave me alone. Get me out of the sun."

"The kids," I say. It is my best argument.

"Fuck the little ones." He talks to me like he knows me, but he does not. Maybe he has seen me. Maybe he has heard about me. Keith talks about me to his supervisor, I am sure, but not in any flattering way. Keith calls me a 'fuck-up.' And surely supervisors talk to the management, and Baptist is management. Maybe in such a way he has heard of me. But I am no Beth, whom everybody knows and who makes us all laugh.

"Let's get into the store," I say. I have his arms and pull him up. I get him to stand and help him stumble inside. "You'll feel better," I say. "Keith is there. Keith will have you singing all the old songs. 'Burger Bear, Burger Bear, Burger-Roo....' Keith will have you dancing. It's your day. It's the first day," I say, "in the rest of your life. I'll be back there on the grill, Keith will be in the window, Mary Lee taking orders and the money, what a team. And Sammy's here, damned good grillman, if not in your league. And you'll be out front dancing for the kids. A hundred kids today, you think? You're the star. You are why we are here, Burger Bear."

Lies, I think, but I must get him inside. If I work, Burger Bear works.

I stand him up, get his arm around my shoulder, and, as he sways on his feet, falling forward, he puts one foot in front of the next. As we step away from the van, I grab Burger Bear's head. Attached to his waist, the rest of his costume drags along as if it is some skin he is shedding.

"Burger Bear, Burger Bear, Burger-Roo," I chant, in tune with the familiar jingle from our television ads. "Burger Bear, Burger Bear, I love you."

He mumbles. I cannot make out his words. That he's sick, he's dying.

He is not dying. Not yet. Maybe his brain is dying. But he is only drunk. I do not want to touch him. He smells of alcohol, and worse. He has vomited somewhere. I don't see him move his feet. He is always a half step behind as I drag him forward, focused on the back door. He breathes faintly and gives off an awful smell. His paws are cold and hard as death.

-7-

"Dead?" Keith says. Then he laughs. "I wish."

"He looks dead," I say.

Baptist lays sprawled along the red clay tiles on the floor. I have half carried him into the store, half dragged him, then propped him against a wall, but Baptist slowly leans to one side like a warm candle melting in the sun until his head touches the floor. His mouth is open, his eyes are closed and the inside of his nose shivers as he breaths. His costume lies lifeless beside him, a shapeless heap of wet fur. Big furry claws are still on his feet, but otherwise he looks small and frail, wearing nothing but his white jockeys and an undershirt.

"Dead drunk, that's all, that fucking lush. Fucking lush," Keith repeats. He says it with disdain. He says it to Baptist who, if he is not dead drunk, can hear. "Fucking asshole lush," Keith says. "Our big day a year. And not yet ten in the morning. Pukes his guts up. Look at that. Now who is going to be Burger Bear for the kids? This guy is funny, right? This guy sells hamburgers, right? This is what I get for my promo budget." Keith sits at his desk. He is not talking to me, but to the stack of neat papers and the money laid out, neat rolls of pennies, nickels and dimes.

Keith is a large man, with a barrel chest and broad shoulders, but his legs are short and bowed slightly outwards. His hair is cut military style—like the dogs he has handled as a soldier in Korea—and he sits erect, with a stiff smile. He always wears his hat. Even at ten in the morning, Keith is wearing the paper Interburger hat—jauntily to one side.

It is his moustache that defines his face—a neat little rectangle pasted across his upper lip, thick and perfectly square, straight so it defines the upper lip of his mouth. It looks too large, to me, for a moustache, more a fence, or a hedge, and his nose sits perched on that hedge and overlooks it. His lips pucker some and he habitually sucks on his moustache from the corner of mouth, from time to time petting it with the tip of his tongue, then combing it with his lower teeth. Below that his chin falls quickly away to a neck so thin it looks inadequate to hold his square head erect.

He looks at me. I avoid his stare. "Should we call an ambulance?" I ask.

"Down the street," he says, avoiding the word Box-A-Burger, "they have a tie-in with a kids' movie. They have rocket ships and monsters. I have a stinking pile of wet fur and this deadbeat."

"He looks awful."

Keith shakes his head. He's counting dollars bills, peeling them off one at a time, wrapping them in sets of twenty-five. "If they had any hair on their ass down at that office, they'd fire him. He's so drunk he couldn't tell a Big Mac from a Burger King."

"Do we need him?" I say.

"Do we need him?" Keith asks. "Him who? That drunk?"

"Can't we do the promo without Burger Bear?" It occurs to me at that moment that I am the next best candidate to put on that stinking costume and spend the day dancing and singing. Keith calms down and straightens his piles of dollar bills, the stacks of pennies.

"There must be a Burger Bear," Keith says. "We have promised our customers Burger Bear, and Burger Bear will be here today." He licks his thumb and counts out a pile of paper currency.

Keith recounts the same money I counted the night before. Keith always unwraps it in the morning, recounts it, rebundles it the way he likes. He is always careful about money and reports.

Keith never rushes. Keith is imperturbable in all that he does, as he is now, sitting in his office making the deposit. He does one thing at a time, and he completes one thing before he starts another. I sit and wait.

"We have to have a Burger Bear," Keith finally says.

"I guess," I say. I can do it, I think. I might be good. It might be fun. But I don't want to. The costume smells awful.

"Get his claws off," Keith says, nodding towards Baptist. "And clean that costume up. Who cares who's inside, as long as it's Burger Bear."

"I don't think it's my size...." I start to say. "And when I sing.... People pay me not to sing. I can sing in the shower. I'm pretty good in the shower," I say, and I laugh a nervous laugh. Keith pays no attention. "But I don't know how we can get shower heads installed by lunchtime."

Keith does not hear me. Maybe I am speaking too softly.

I pray, 'Let it not be me, Jesus, not me. Not a clown.' I imagine being buried in that Burger Bear outfit, hot, hairy, itchy, gagging on the stench. Were that not enough, I imagine dancing, and laughing, and playing with little kids who come in expecting the happy dancing bear they have seen on TV. I will have to tease them, entertain them, be nice to them, live up to the image of Burger Bear, "as happy as a BurgerRoo." Keith will be watching me. He will stand behind the steam table on the back line, peer out as he sucks on his moustache, and I will be under his godawful glare as I dance.

I hate little kids. They show up in droves, hungry and expecting a perfect television bear. And, at Interburger they become a mob, driven into a frenzy by mothers, coupons, and fast food. They fill their little faces with food, chewing with their mouths open, and spitting, and sneezing, and dribbling. Seeking a monster, they become monsters. We make them so. We think that will make them loyal customers.

The parents are as bad. Their mothers drive them here, push them into the toddling crowd, tell them how to beg for coupons, egg them on to dance and squeal. Everything here is darling. And the Bear is expected to dance and cavort, to hold the little dears, to be the best and biggest monster of all time, role model monster, horrible and harmless, singing to the little brats, holding them, hugging them, autographing their french fry bags with his paw, giving away free food.

I can do it. I can perform if I have to. But I don't want to.

"I have no intention of putting you out there," Keith says. He rises, zips the money bag shut, then tucks it in his belt. "I'm going to the bank. Sammy will be here any time. Sammy will be Burger Bear. You," he says, looking at me, "will work with me, take Sammy's place on the grill."

"You don't want me to be Burger Bear?" I say to make sure I hear correctly.

Then, to my surprise, I feel disappointed. I would be great. And Sammy is only a grillman, after all. I am a born American. Sammy is only two years out of Lebanon. What does he know about our culture, our kids, and the American communion of fast food?

I do not want to be Burger Bear, but I want Keith to want me. He should at least ask me.

"Oh, god no," Keith says, as he takes off his paper hat, folds it neatly, puts it in his desk drawer. "No," he says, shaking his head, as if to confirm his doubts. "Not at all," he says. "I've never found the Burger Bear in you, and that, buddy boy, has been a disappointment."

With this he puts on a baseball hat, adjusts it down on his head just so, in that same jaunty cock he has when he wears the paper hat, and then he leaves by the back door for the bank.

-8-

Except for his forced breathing and the flapping of the membranes in his nose, Baptist has lain quietly on the red tile floor just inside Keith's office. He sounds like a hospital respirator. His lips are parted, his tongue pokes out a corner of his mouth, and he labors to inhale, in, then out. His thin face is bluish gray, and he looks old. I have always thought of Baptist as big, especially when he plays the part of the Bear, but I know the furry costume exaggerates his size. He looks bigger in disguise. Near naked, he looks more like a giant guppy. His eyes are closed. He has brought the smell of gin and sour food into Keith's office.

"Whoa," Sammy says, appearing at the office door. Sammy is a big man, over three hundred pounds, and he fills the office doorway. He wears warm-up pants, as always held up by a cord, and his T-shirt hangs over his stomach.

Sammy is our day grillman, and he arrives on schedule minutes before the store opens. Sammy is barely twenty years old, with a heavy beard. His olive complexion betrays his Middle Eastern roots.

Sammy has been in America for two years. He came here, he says, to tend Arabian horses on a farm owned by a Saudi outside town. But the horses contracted hoof and mouth, were quarantined for a month, and put down. Sammy had been their trainer, but now, like a half dozen other friends from the Middle East he is here without work or money. He cannot go home. The Saudis blame him for the loss of their horses. He is certain the Saudis will kill him.

Sammy works as much as Keith allows. Sammy loves his job, but Keith makes him leave when his shift is up. Sammy would work doubles every day, if asked. Sammy dreams he is going to make a fortune in America and return to Lebanon to open up his own restaurant, perhaps a chain. The "Awful Falafel" he calls it. Sammy says it sounds clever in Arabic. He tells me that in Lebanon fat is beautiful. He thinks it will be an honor to introduce fast food to a country that admires fat.

I like Sammy. He is the gentlest person I know. He has an indomitable outlook, always positive, always happy. He never complains.

"Who's that?" Sammy asks as he enters the back line. He steps around Baptist who lies sprawled on the floor.

"Baptist," I say. "Our director of marketing."

"It's Burger Bear," Sammy says. He points to the costume. Maybe, I think, Sammy had never seen Burger Bear without his costume.

"Burger Bear," I say, in the way of a full explanation. "The man inside."

"Oh," Sammy says. "I know." He kneels down and touches the costume, the boots, the gloves, the skin and head. Sammy nods, full of belief and admiration. Nothing in America surprises him. He has often said it before. "This is a wonderful country. This is a wonderful costume."

"It stinks."

"Today," Sammy says, touching his chest, "I am Burger Bear. Keith has asked."

"We got to get that thing cleaned."

"Today," Sammy says, touching his chest with his fingertips, "I the Bear." He looks up at me.

"It's not fair," I say. But Sammy is not listening. He has a dreamy look in his eyes.

"I am so happy," Sammy says. "I love America."

There is no reasoning with Sammy now. "We can wash it out...."

"It's almost eleven," Mary Lee says, peeking around the grill. "Where's Keith?"

"At the bank," I say.

"Who's cooking?"

"Me, I guess."

"Well, good God," Mary Lee says. "You better turn the grill on. They're coming. The customers are circling."

In a flash she is back on the front line. Mary Lee is everywhere. Keith has trained her well, with the result that the closer it comes to opening, the closer we are to panic.

She never stops moving. In ninety minutes Mary Lee has wiped down the counters, front line and back, put away utensils the night crew had washed, wiped spots off the windows, refilled the salt and pepper shakers, filled the napkin holders, rebuilt the stainless steel shake machine from the parts the night crew had disassembled and washed, filled the shake machine with mix and turned it on to begin the endless flow of aerated shakes. She has chopped a day's supply of lettuce and sliced two trays of tomatoes. She has readied the registers, too, loaded each with the exact amount of change as prescribed in the manual. In this way when the counter girls come, they waste no time setting up. But no matter how perfect her routine, no matter how fast she works, nothing is ever quite ready enough for Mary Lee. Nothing is ever perfectly right. She lives in fear that she has overlooked something. Keith has trained her well.

"We open at eleven," she says, repeating the mantra she repeats all morning. "And they're expecting Burger Bear. Wackhoff's coming, too." Mary Lee passes by the office door and then is gone.

"The supervisor?" I ask. Wackhoff supervises this store and a dozen others.

"Wouldn't you know?" Mary Lee says, passing by the other way. "He'll come in and find we aren't ready. I don't know when he's going to be here. I don't know when...." She is still talking, but I cannot hear her.

Sammy has pulled the boots off Baptist's feet.

"I'll wash that thing out," I say. "It stinks."

The Burger Bear contraption is a mishmash of buttons, snaps, wires, straps and elastic. I drag it to the sink and clean it as best I can. The more I clean, however, the wetter it gets and the heavier. I leave it hanging over the sink to dry.

"Good luck, Sammy," I say. "It's soggy." Water drips to the floor.

"I am the Bear," Sammy still says, smiles, pats his chest with one hand, but he hardly talks to me.

Good luck, I think. As I scrape the grill and get ready for lunch, I dream of being Burger Bear, how I would play the part. I could have done it, I think. Maybe I should have. It might have been fun to try. I can sing well enough. Who hears anything over all those squealing kids? As for dancing, well, I both waltz and jitterbug. I can do the Elvis thing with my hips which kids think is so cute when they see Burger Bear doing it. I would find the cutest little girl, one who is pleasant and awestruck by the Bear, and waltz her around a time or two. I would be good. I could—if I wanted to—be damned good. Now I regret I have not said something to Keith, volunteered for the job. Maybe Baptist would have been grateful and given me a job, something in the main office, or something in marketing, away from Keith, and away from High Hawk Road.

In the office, I think, is where I should be. Not behind a grill on High Hawk Road. In the central office I could develop my ideas. Someone there will hear and understand. I have ideas. New items for a better menu. Ways of decorating the units. A new logo. An ad campaign. I excel in ideas. Not in sweeping floors. Anything would be better than working for Keith, standing over a hot grill, frying meat and being yelled at. Cheese and salt and pickles and heat, the smell of grease in my nostrils, buns toasting too much on the grill, meat burnt, Keith on my ass. Oh, I have been trained. I know what today is going to be. It is lunch, and a Friday, and a Burger Bear day, and Keith on my ass before I'm even awake.

Out there, in the costume, I would be the show. In control. In the middle of the lunch rush, I would stop everything. Who would question me—Burger Bear? I would stand and talk, say what I want, and be heard. I would make news. 'Don't eat this crap,' I would say. The children would stop all they were doing.

'Burger Bear is a fake,' I would say. 'The real Burger Bear is a man, and he is drunk, and passed out in the back. And that man back there,' I would say, pointing with my paw, pointing to the little window above the steam table, where Keith can be seen, his face looking out, his jaw agape, frozen as I speak, 'He is the biggest ass hole in the world. Look at him. We are what we eat, boys and girls. What we eat is what sustains us, and you are nourished on his fries, fed by his meat, quenched with his soda pop.... And it is crap!'

Burger Bear in revolt. I am famous. I make the Channel 5 news.

I should have said something to Keith. I should have said something to Sammy. Now it is too late. I lay ten meat patties on the grill, two rows of five. Those are the little guys. Then eight quarter pounders, in rows of four—soul of the BurgerRoo. The grill is hot, the meat sizzles, and I smell the first grease of the day.

A dark wet streak on the floor follows Sammy as he drags his costume behind him. He heads to the bathroom to change. The costume smells worse now than before. Like a babe in birth, he is slow being born.

-9-

Mary Lee pokes her head around the corner. "Five minutes, fellas. I'm giving the girls their registers." She takes the keys from Keith and carries out the money trays. Mary Lee is calm, like just before the storm.

I have put on my apron and stand in front of the grill, ready for my part. I am putting up the build—that assortment of sandwiches we keep ready to serve during the rush.

"You haven't seen it yet," Keith says to me. He is standing with his hands on the counter, staring through the window at the girls up front. This will be his station for the next few hours. From there he will oversee the whole store. "You have been here an hour and you haven't seen it. I've trained you for over a year, and you know nothing."

"What's that?" I ask. "I don't know what you're saying." Is he asking if my hat is on right, but it is on well enough. I wear a clean apron, as I am supposed to. The meat is where it is supposed to be, on a shelf beside the grill, stacks of patties separated by paper, ready to cook. The grill is hot, the exact temperature recommended in the manual, or near enough. The patties are frying. I have not yet burned them. The pickles, the cheese, the fries are ready. A rack of buns are handy. I will rip open the plastic bags covering the buns as I need them and drop them on the grill to toast. My hands are clean, I am ready, I am here. What is wrong? What feather does Keith have up his ass?

"Follow me." Keith motions with his finger for me to follow him to the lobby.

It is a simple lobby, the same as most fast food restaurants in America, and identical to every other Interburger. Three glass walls encase a series of tables bolted to the floor, some along the sides, some free standing, and most with stools with metal backs that are bolted down tight. The floor is red tile, easy to clean. Everything in the lobby is brown, or orange—light brown, dark brown, light orange and dark orange, Burger Bear colors. The floors are clean. At night my night crew sweep the floors, then mop them. A broom is still there, leaning against a wall. The little twerps should have put it away, and I should have made them do it, but we had been in a hurry last night, I anxious for my time with the lovely Beth.

"What do you see?" Keith asks.

"What do I see?" I repeat. He does not look at me, but around the room, at nothing in particular. I wonder what he is seeing. The tables are clean. Salt shakers are on the tables where they should be. Windows have been polished, fingerprints and smudges removed from the doors. My crew has done well, I think. Outside, no litter in the drive, no trash against the fence. "Everything looks fine."

People outside are waiting to get in, sitting in their cars, sitting on picnic benches and by the door.

Keith avoids looking at me. His jaws are not clenched, but they are set firm, a distant look on his face—indifferent, patient—clues that something is wrong that I should find it.

The counters are clean. The stainless steel as polished as ever. Keith keeps a good unit, and neat despite its age. He trains us to keep everything just so.

Napkins are stocked. Condiments, the shake machine, coffee pots, all are as they should be. The coffee is perking. Mary Lee has turned the shake machine on and it is humming, frosted on the front as the mix inside is freezing. The store is about to open, and we are ready as best I can tell.

But then I get it. Of course it is there. I wonder how I missed it, how I failed to see it the night before, how I failed to know that Keith would see it.

"Would it be the broom?" I ask. Of course it is.

"The broom," Keith says, but he acts surprised. Then he waits. He could say something, but he waits for me to say something more.

"It doesn't belong there, does it?" I say.

"The broom?" he repeats. "Well, no, I guess it doesn't," he says. "I guess when we are finished with the broom, we put it back where it belongs."

"I guess we do," I say.

"I guess we will."

So that is it. I take the broom and carry it back to the rear of the store where I hang it on its hook.

Saying nothing, Keith follows me, then heads into his office. I do not follow him. I stand outside and wait. He does not look back.

Grease bubbles through the patties of meat, and I flip them to cook on the other side.

Keith re-emerges, wearing his orange apron and paper hat. He leans against the counter, hunches down, and stares out over the steam table and into the lobby. Mary Lee unlocks the front door. One more morning has morphed into lunchtime, and the rush begins.

Noon

- 1 -

"Let's cook," Keith says with finality. He stands staring through the window. I am at the grill. It is cool and polished smooth, like sanded wood. Smooth as a baby's butt. It feels sacrilegious to dirty it. I have my own apron on, and lean against the grill as the patties cook. Grease runs into the trays in front and back, channelling the grease to the buckets underneath. I have a pan of meat patties on one side, large bricks of sliced cheese beside it, and racks of buns behind.

"Let's move," Keith says. "Give me another sixteen and twenty. They're coming in." Keith loves this time of day—the beginning of lunch, our biggest and busiest hour at High Hawk Road. He forgets me in the frenzy. He forgets himself. We become a chain that processes food. He expects it to work perfectly.

He sees everything from his place on the back line, paper hat cocked to one side, bending down to peer through the window to see the front line as well. He sees every order taken, ever sandwich sold, every nickel dropped into the register. Nothing escapes him—special orders, standard orders, the customers new and regular. He garnishes every sandwich that goes out. He is excited.

He remains excited, too, until the last penny is counted, and he has totaled up the day's take, compared today's figures to the day before, called his numbers in to the office, compared them to the other stores, computed how well he had done this week, and this month, and this year, compared them to this time last year, and this week to last week. Better is better. Better is always better. Better is always expected. Keith hates to be disappointed.

It is not money that matters. It isn't his money, after all. It is the game, and when sales are up or down, whether the performance at High Hawk Road is better or worse, it is as if Keith himself has been drawn out on the charts, how he has grown, gotten better, or been disappointed. Keith sees it as if he is being judged, as if some part of him is judging all the rest. We are just an old pair of shoes he wears to get some place he wants to go—appendages that will someday wear out and fail him. Shoes he will have to replace.

For me I want nothing more than to be as invisible as an old pair of shoes.

"Sixteen, twenty," I echo. The grillman repeats the orders that come down from the window.

The first fresh meat patties stick to the grill as I slap them down, the little guys in rows of fives, the big guys—the quarter pounders—in sets of four, and in seconds they are sizzling. Juice in the patties rises to the top, grease bubbles through, four rows of five, a "twenty." Then four rows of four quarter pounders, "sixteen." I cut the little guys clean off the grill with my spat which is as sharp as a razor, a grilled patina on their cooked side, flipping them quickly and with grace so they line up in a new row, the cooked side up and the raw side taking its turn on the grill.

I pull buns apart and lay them down in rows to toast on the grill. Half of the grill is for buns, half for meat.

"Cheese on eight."

"Cheese eight," I repeat. The buns are toasted. I pull the small ones up. Then the twenty. I lay them on trays, heels on one side, crowns on the other, and lay the patties on the heels and ship them down to Keith who garnishes them—ketchup, squirt, squirt, mustard, squirt, onions exactly sixteen pieces, two pickles on the small, three for the big guys—then he assembles the buns and meat, and wraps them and flicks them down the steam table to where the girls out front pick them up and put them in the bags. I turn twenty small patties with a flick, flick, flick, flick, flipping them so they land in a straight line inches to the right—four rows of five patties each, flip, flip, flip. Then the sixteen, cutting them from the grill with a swipe of the spat, swoosh, then turning them, flip, flip, flip. Salting everything. Small patties on the buns, and the tray down to Keith. Big buns up.

"Lay twenty. Cheese on eight."

Two slices of cheese on eight of the quarters. Big patties up, tray to the window.

"Cheese on ten."

"Twenty, cheese eight, cheese ten," I echo.

I cover the buns with the patties, then slide them down to Keith. He makes the singles, doubles, with cheese, without. He constructs the wholly mysterious, completely inimitable BurgerRoo—two small patties, two cheese, three pickles, sixteen pieces of onion, two shots of ketchup squirt, squirt, one shot of mystery sauce (much like Thousand Island dressing, a hint of mayonnaise, like the guys down the street use) glop, on a sesame seed bun. Quarter pounders cheesed. Quarter pounders up. Quarter pounders wrapped and pushed down the steam table trays to the front line.

Hobbles is out front, always our first customer of the day, at Mary Lee's register, asking for a fresh cheeseburger.

"It's got to be fresh," Hobbles says every day, like he worries we keep cheeseburgers overnight.

"Hey, Hobbles," Keith says. "Cheeseburger coming up. Sixteen, twenty," to me.

Hobbles is harbinger of the day, our rooster crowing the rising of the burger shack. Keith peers through the steamy square cut between the walls, over the chutes above the steam table. Hobbles nods and smiles. Keith wraps the sandwiches. He is quick, skillful, and he brushes the sandwiches down the chutes with a gentle flip of his finger. More customers come in. Girls grab the burgers and put them in bags.

"Well," I say, "let's go, then. Sixteen. Twenty." I breathe deep and deal out the patties of meat and buns. I flip the little ones. The grill is full of meat and buns, grease dancing, and the smell of cooking meat rises from the steam and is slowly sucked into the hood. Grease melts away from the cooking meat, catches in the filters, drips down, joins a flow to the trays around the grill, and from there dripping into the buckets below. I am moving fast.

"Sixteen, four doubles. Another twenty, half stacked."

How much can I do? How fast can I cook? Can I keep up with Keith? He with me? I become one with the job, my movements automatic, no thoughts at all. Every move is desperate. Every move is automatic. I have no other thoughts. The crowd out front is growing. The lines in front of the register grow longer. We move faster. I am keeping up.

Then something happens out of place, a noise out front, a presence behind me, a presence standing beyond Keith, large and dark. I am sweating and the sweat gets in my eyes. The splattering grease stings my hands. My fingers are numb from touching the grill. I wipe my forehead with the sleeve of my shirt.

He is smiling. Burger Bear has one expression, a smile. He claps his hands—one paw thumping against the other. Then, for us alone, because he is not yet out front, but on the back line, dancing on one foot, then on the other, then back and forth. Then his arms go up, back and forth with his dancing, and he mutters, "Ho, ho, ho."

He smells. Of what? Wet fur, yes. Lebanon. Horses. Gin. Puke.

"That's Santa Claus," Keith says. "A bear growls. He's hungry." Keith watches and laughs but he does not miss a move as he wraps sandwiches. "Sixteen."

Sammy stands on one foot and hopped, turning around in the narrow space in the back line. He pulls at his feet, and tugs at his paws, and head, until he gets them to fit snug, then he dances again, on one foot, around and around, then on the other. Sammy laughs. I laugh. He is good. He claps his hands and practices a roar. He is Burger Bear laughing.

"Go for it," I say. "Sixteen."

"Another sixteen, twenty. Eight and ten with cheese. That's it," Keith says. He walks around Sammy, inspecting him from claw to paw. "That's Burger Bear." Keith wipes his hands and pulls a sheaf of coupons from his back pocket. "You're going to be great," he says. "You're going to be one of the great ones." He adjusts Burger Bear's head a bit, pulls a flap of fur down over Sammy's neck, adjusts the shoulder strings and fixes the Velcro. He does it in an approving way. "Dance, Sammy," he says. "Dance, Burger Bear. The kids will love you."

"Burger Bear is dead," I say. "God save Burger Bear." I am laughing. I am smiling. He isn't bad. I could have done it, I could have been the Burger Bear, but Sammy isn't bad at all.

"r-r-r-r-RRR-owl-l-l-l-l."

"Sixteen, twenty, eight and ten cheese, echo."

"Hey, no fooling like that," Keith says. "Don't scare the little shits. Another sixteen, another twenty."

I slide a tray down, a tray, a tray, another tray. Buns, meat. "Sixteen, twenty. Echo on the cheese."

"Cheese 'em all."

When Sammy reaches up, like a bear on his hind legs reaching for the sky with his paws, he stretches eight foot tall or more, a giant to a four-year-old. Like some mother hen preening her chicks, Keith looks him over for a loose button or an undone strap.

"Maybe you shouldn't say anything at all," Keith says. "Remember, you are a bear. Not a human. You growl, but growl nice. Like you ate a BurgerRoo and you liked it. Make 'em hungry. Hamburgers. Cheeseburgers. Burger Bear's fries. You got the coupons, Burger Bear," Keith says. "Get their mothers to buy. And only one to a kid, okay?"

Keith stuffs a few more coupons into a secret pocket on the costume. Burger Bear holds a few coupons awkwardly in his paws. "r-r-r-r-RRR-owl-l-l-l-l."

"No, Sammy. Say it, Ham-bur-ger-r-r-r," I say. "Chee-e-e-se-bur-r-r-r-r-ger."

"Burger me," Sammy says, but his voice is muffled and seems far away.

"Don't say that," Keith says. He has a look of panic for a moment. "And for god's sake," he says, turning to me, "don't fuck around. Sixteen." He shakes his head, turns to Sammy and pats his still damp fur.

"Sixteen."

"Go, Sammy," Keith says, turning him around and nudging him out. "Go get 'em," he says. He pushes Burger Bear through the narrow way between the fryers and the back counter.

"Shellaine," Keith says to one of the counter girls. "Work with Burger Bear. Burger Bear needs a girlfriend. To keep him in line."

Burger Bear stretches his arms and roars at Shellaine who has just clocked in. Shellaine is night crew, mine, my favorite. But she loves to work and during the summer Keith often calls her in on busy days. This is such a day.

Shellaine works hard, and she is easily bored, and she imagines she is qualified to run the place, at least at night when I am in charge. She probably is. Sunday nights, in fact, she takes my place, in charge for the slowest night of the week and my night off. Shellaine is never satisfied with doing any one job for long. She always wants something to do — to fry, clean, count money, work out front, run errands, wash windows, paint the bears on the roof. Nothing proves too difficult, too dirty, for Shellaine. Today she wears her orange uniform, which does nothing to detract from her subtle young beauty. Half an American Indian, she is a long distance runner in school. At work she is cocky, boyish, sarcastic and funny, and that silly uniform disguises none of her.

"Do you like our Burger Bear?" Keith asks her. "Doesn't he look like the real thing?"

Shellaine stares at him, peering at him as if she to find a spot where she can see who is there. But no such place exists in all that soggy fur. "Who is that?" she asks. "Is that you, Sammy?"

"Don't let him get too crazy," Keith says. He is at his window wrapping sandwiches. "Thirty-two and twenty, half with cheese."

"And if he does?" she asks. She is about a third Sammy's size. "Then what?"

"Thirty two and twenty," I echo.

"Stop him, of course," Keith says. "Whack his butt." Keith demonstrates by spanking a BurgerRoo, wrapping it with a single motion as if he is putting it in diapers and flicking it down the chute out front. Keith smiles. He is having fun, while I am sweating and am already dead tired. Shellaine smiles, too. She and Keith are different, but they get along.

There is too much meat on the grill for me to handle. Even when Keith slows down for a moment or two, I cannot keep up. I have not been paying attention, some buns have burned, a patty of meat has slipped into the grease tray. I am falling behind. Keith is laying the buns for me—the grillman's job, but no matter how fast I work, how much I do, I am falling behind.

Shellaine smiles as she puts on her hat and heads to the lobby, following Burger Bear, happy to be doing something different today. She is fearless.

"Cook!" Keith says, turning to me. The meat is overcooking. I rush to keep from falling further behind, but I stay behind. "Pay attention to what you're doing. We need another thirty-two."

I cook as fast as I can, faster than ever before. I fry, I flip, and I cover the buns and scoot them down the line to Keith whose only comments are more numbers divisible by four or five, instructions for cheese, and then, soon enough, ever more irritable remarks. "You're losing it, Chris. Goddamn it. Double two quarters with cheese. Ten on sixteen. Another eight."

Then, "God damn it, can't you cook?"

Then, "That's over cooked, you're ruining it, Chris. The cheese, it's a mess. And we haven't even started."

It is a mess. The cheese has melted and burned on the grill. I like the smell. But enough of that and the grill will be dirty and not hot enough to fry properly. Coated with a film of burnt food, the patties do not fry as the book requires. Hamburgers must fry, not bake.

"Your buns," Keith says. "You are burning your buns! Lay down sixteen, twenty-four, no thirty-two!"

Too much salt. More meat, more buns, more cheese. More meat, more buns, more cheese. Clean the grill. The grill's a mess. The meat's overcooked. You're baking it now, not frying. Do I have to say it again. Do I have to do it for you.

Time barely passes. This is hell and it can go forever. Punishment for crimes I fail to remember. I am falling behind. Can I fall so far behind that time goes retrograde and day returns to morning?

-2-

Sammy is a marvel as Burger Bear. He needs none of the padding that comes in the costume. At first he navigates with difficulty around the tables bolted to the lobby floor. He steps carefully around the children so small and eager to get between his feet. But then, stumbling about is Burger Bear, is it not? And that concern in his eyes, buried in the furry head, concern and fear for doing right, that comes across as a hungry look—pure Burger Bear.

The kids are slow in arriving, which gives Burger Bear a chance to warm up, to test his new self. The first kid shows up at half past eleven—a little boy of three or four, wearing a baseball hat, and pants and shirt freshly washed and pressed. He sees Burger Bear and screams. The second shows up moments later. But Burger Bear ignores him. He does not look their way, but lets them—like dogs—stand and admire his huge, furry self, size him up. Then they venture closer. Burger Bear talks with Shellaine, dances a subtle step or two, but not for the kids, not looking at the kids, and the kids step closer. One finally reaches out and touches the Bear. Burger Bear still ignores him, talks with Shellaine, sings a little song, but not to the kids. Cautiously the kids step up to touch the Bear. And at last one kid, an older kid steps forward and embraces his great bear leg. "I love you, Burger Bear. I love you."

Then Sammy begins. He turns to face them and laughs and dances. He is a big and harmless little bear, not the made-up monster from television or movies. Not a comic book creature. But Burger Bear alive. No picture on a soda cup, or a tin bear on the roof. Not a picture on a bus, or a Saturday morning cartoon. Burger Bear alive! Burger Bear here! And real, and breathing, and dancing. Burger Bear faces them, standing between the fryers and the front line, broad in the beam, furry, tall so the top of his head brushes the hamburger mobiles that dangle from the ceiling.

"Hello, little boys, little girls," Burger Bear says. "Welcome to my party. Welcome to my home. Welcome to my kitchen. Did your mommy bring you in for a little BurgerRoo? Hoo, hoo, hoo." A little boy screams, but not out of fear, but from surprise, and love, and excitement. He runs towards Burger Bear and grabs his other leg and will not let go. Thus Burger Bear hobbles around with sixty pounds of little boy wrapped around each leg.

"Now, look there, sweetheart," his mother says. "You mustn't hold on to the bear like that. Only talk to him, and tell him you love him, then let's get our coupons and food and go."

"Free fries, little ones, free burgers." Burger Bear holds out coupons, and many hands reach out to grab them. Bear hobbles about, dragging children along.

Soon more kids arrive. The restaurant is full. Cars circle the lot outside looking for places to park. Some park in the Lucky Spoon next door and walk their children down to the highway and then up the drive to get free coupons.

A mother holds a screaming boy by the hand and tells Burger Bear, "He's a good boy." The boy holds on to his mother, but he looks from that safe perch wide-eyed at Burger Bear.

"I know," Burger Bear says from deep inside.

Then the boy reaches out and grabs his nose, which would hurt had it been real. Burger Bear hops away and around. He dances. There are so many other boys and girls to see and sing to. What is Sammy thinking, I wonder. Shellaine pries the children off Burger Bear's feet, but as they are forced to let go, others latch on.

"Hi, little boy," Shellaine says. "Are you hungry? Want a BurgerRoo?"

He looks at her for a moment with wide eyes, but turns to the leg he embraces and sinks his teeth into the fur. He only has a mouth full of fur, not Sammy, but he looks like he is enjoying the thought of the pain he should be causing.

"Burger Bear loves little boys," Sammy says, then he hops from one leg to the other and he begins to sing old tunes. His hopping finally shakes the boys loose, and they fall to the floor and start crying. Free to dance at last, Burger Bear does, and the noise from the crowd drowns out the childish wailing.

"Burger Bear, Burger Bear..." He begins the song that everyone knows, especially the kids, from the many television commercials, and everyone chimes in. The lines in front of the registers are growing, the lobby is full, the cash registers are ringing. Outside cars circle the lot looking for parking space. I fry. I am falling behind.

"Burger Bear, Burger Bear, we love you.
Burger Bear, Burger Bear, good to chew.
Mommy-o, daddy-o, treat me, do.
Gimm-a, gimm-a, BurgerRoo!"

Not just Burger Bear, not just Shellaine, not just the staff who sang as they fetched the orders, not just Keith, and not just me, but everyone in the store gets caught up in the song. It is an anthem. It is a psalm.

Perhaps it is Sammy hopping back and forth from one leg to the other, then back again that terrifies the children. He is an unsteady monster as he dances and sings. Shellaine stands beside him and holds him steady, guiding him along, but the lobby shivers as he shifts his weight. He hits a few tables, and the children stand safely a few feet away.

One boy cries constantly, then stops. Then, he closes his eyes and cries. He sits with his mother at a table and his sandwich grows cold. Burger Bear sees the bawl baby, and as he approaches, the herd of kids follow, some still clutching his legs, others pulling at his fur.

"Boo," Burger Bear says, and he laughs, and all the kids around him laugh, except the bawler who makes fists with his hands, his eyes wide open, and his face frozen in terror. The Bear dances and laughs, but the red-eyed weeper does not laugh, does not move. The Bear dances again, hopping from one foot to the other. Nothing changes but the center of gravity.

His mother finally stands and picks her boy up. Apologies in her eyes, she smiles and leaves, her mess of half-eaten lunch still on the table. With a shrug, and a hop from the left foot to the right, and the right foot to the left, Burger Bear dances, breaking the tension, and the kids are squealing again.

The crowd renews itself every fifteen minutes. The old crowd leaves, a new crowd arrives for food and to see the dancing bear. Sammy is singing now. The tunes sound foreign, off tone and alien, but are perfect for this friendly monster with a fist full of coupons.

Then I hear the whack. I wipe away sweat running down my face, and look around the corner out front. Shellaine is poking Burger Bear, prodding him to move this way and that with a yardstick she has found. She whacks Sammy on the rear. "Dance!" she orders. "Sing!"

And Sammy dances and sings on cue. She is his trainer. His tamer. Now the kids laugh as Shellaine beats him with her quirt—a newspaper folded up into a tube, and they clap to the tune she makes him sing. The words are foreign, Lebanese, but they sing along without understanding. Keith is wrapping sandwiches, firing them down the steam table chutes with deliberate flicks of his fingers, looking up from time to time, looking out, sucking on his moustache and giggling as well.

"Dance," Shellaine says. Whack. And the kids are giggling, holding their hands over their mouths. It is not yet even noon.

-3-

"Do they like me, do you think?" Sammy asks. "Do you think they really like me?" Sammy honestly does not know. Buried inside so much fur and padding, his senses numbed by the gloves and headpiece, he cannot tell if the kids are laughing or heckling. "Do I do right?"

Sammy has retreated to the back line to rest. Out front the kids are screaming for him to come back. Shellaine has stayed with the kids and she is promising Burger Bear will return.

"I don't think they like me."

"They love you, Sammy," Keith says. He wraps sandwiches, places them in the center of a square piece of wrap, then, with a single simple twist, the sandwich is properly wrapped inside a paper, neat and tight, then flicked down the steam table tray.

"I don't know," Sammy says. He has the headpiece off. His hair is wet and laid flat on his head. "I don't know what to do. I've never been a bear. What does a good bear do? How do you know if you're doing it right? I don't know."

"You do it right," Keith says.

Sammy sits on the small chair in a corner near the freezer where it is cool. He looks overheated. The chair had a small round base and a heart-shaped back, which his big fur butt seems to have swallowed. He holds his bear head between his knees as he slumps forward. Keith drops fries into the hot grease, and the grease foams and boils. He garnishes two trays of toasted buns, squirt, squirt, then squirt, then plop and plink. Keith has a genius for garnishing and wrapping. And he is calm now as he will be throughout the rest of the rush. It is seconds until noon. The big rush has yet to begin.

"You are Burger Bear," Keith says.

"I don't even know what to do."

"Whatever you do is right," Keith says. "That's the beauty of being the Bear. Whatever you do is Burger Bear. Whatever Burger Bear does is right. You create him by putting on that costume. They don't care out there about anything else, just that you are. They come to see Burger Bear. You can walk out there now with your head in your hands, take off your paws, speak in Lebanese, and they will say, that's Burger Bear. You got them. They believe in Burger Bear. They believe in you."

"Burger Bear, Burger Bear, Burger-Roo...." I laugh, but no one notices me. Sixteen. Ten. Another ten. Keith—squirt, squirt....

"Do you think?" Sammy asks. "Don't they want the real thing?" he says, looking to where Baptist lays, his bare feet sticking out of Keith's office. He is still on his back and passed out. "Did you see them scream? One kid, he got sick. I don't know. You let me cook. Let Chris go out there."

"You're great," I say. My grill is a vast plate of steaming meat patties, buns toasting, cheese melting, but I want to encourage Sammy, too, to make him feel good. I am happy he is out there, and not me. But I could have done it.

"What's real?" Keith asks. He talks to Sammy over his shoulder as he wraps sandwiches and flips them down the trays. "What's real is what's here. And you're here. And he's gone," he says, nodding to Baptist on the floor. "You're doing great. Thirty-six, eighteen, and a twenty on twenty. Hurry up, Chris, you're falling behind."

I am. Patties are burning on the grill. The buns are over-toasting. I flip a set, then gather up the buns and scoop the meat out on them, scrap the grill clean in two quick strokes, then lay another set of sixteen, four rows of four. But I am not keeping up. Our early build is gone. The girls out front are standing at the window looking back, asking for more, asking for special orders, looking daggers at Keith, who looks daggers at me. They know, as I know, Keith is not the problem. I am working faster than ever. I am working as fast as I can.

"I don't know no English songs, no American dances," Sammy says. "Do you think the little American kids like me? Really?" His elbows on his knees, Sammy's head hangs low. His doubts are real.

"I don't care what you sing," Keith says. "They don't either. Little shits. What do they know? The Muffin Man? Hey Diddle Diddle. Sing anything. Sing in Arabic. Sing about horses. They're kids. They don't know. And their mothers want the coupons. If you start to lose, if you think you're in trouble, just give out the coupons. They love that shit."

Out front Shellaine is promising a growing mob of kids that Burger Bear will reemerge, but they seem dubious. They sneak around the corners of the counter and shout for Burger Bear.

"We want Burger Bear! We want Burger Bear!"

Shellaine is passing out coupons freely. Dozens of dozens of kids are in the store, and more arrive every moment. Never has High Hawk been so full. I have a grill covered with meat and buns, an iron raft of steamy cooking burgers so full I barely have room to flip the patties. Even Keith is working flat out now. He never breaks his calm demeanor, but he is quieter than usual. He can chew me out, but we are in trouble. I am afraid.

"You're losing it, Chris," he says. He does not sound angry. "Sixteen, no, make that thirty-two. And forty." Outside kids are hanging on Shellaine. Customers are lined up six deep in front of the registers. The lot is full of cars and more cars are coming in.

"Should I stay back here and cook?" Sammy asks. He has risen. Even he can see that I am losing the battle. For a moment he hesitates about coming to help.

"Twenty more," Keith says. "Twenty more. No, forty. Half with cheese. Twelve Roos. Fries down. You are the best Burger Bear we got, Sammy. Get out there now. We do what we can do."

"Burger Bear! Burger Bear...! We want Burger Bear!" The kids are chanting and getting louder. Keith is cool, but there is a tone in his voice. It is calm, but with an edge. Rest is over for Sammy.

"Am I good?" Sammy asks. He is really asking. "I mean, am I doing it right?"

"You got it," Keith says. He turns to face Sammy and pats his own heart with a hand that holds a BurgerRoo. "In the heart, Sammy." He says it with sincerity. He stops completely doing his important work to focus entirely for a moment on Sammy. "Let Burger Bear come from the heart. Do the Bear for them."

There is silence between them for a moment, and communication beyond words. Sammy looks down, then breaths deep, as if drawing in the first breath of the day.

"Okay?" Keith asks.

"Okay," Sammy says. "You got it, boss." It is a quiet affirmation, but firm. Sammy has made up his mind. Keith has touched him.

"That's good," Keith says, turning back to the pandemonium at the window. "Now get the fuck out there and show those little bastards a bear." Keith's hands are a marvel of deftness. There is no wasted movement in them, no hesitation and the sandwiches are created, wrapped and flicked down the chute with such speed I wonder if some spirit is helping him. Squirt, squirt, squirt.

Sammy looks into the dark depths of the great bear head, holds it up, then pulls it down over his own. He snaps the buttons and smooths down the Velcro, and stands. Sammy has disappeared into the Bear. The Bear has swallowed Sammy.

On the frontline customers buy sandwiches as fast as we get them out the window. The counter girls are waiting for sandwiches and fries, calling back special orders to Keith, sandwiches with this and that, and others without something normally added, ones with twice the normal something else. Sammy puts on his gloves, pulls on his paws, and stands, but his shoulders sag, perhaps from resignation, perhaps from the weight of the Bear. This time, unlike the first time, though, he makes his way gracefully through that narrow channel between the fryers and the grill. And when he emerges, alive, renewed, he is greeted with a roar of squeals and giggles. They have expected him, and they are pleased. For a moment, thank god, the distraction takes the pressure off me as I race to keep up with their voracious appetite for burgers. The crowd moves away from the registers and followed the dancing, singing bear again.

My grill is hot. The hamburgers spatter grease all about. My hands are stinging with tiny blisters. But I redouble my effort. The real rush is now on. I cut the patties from the grill and flip them so they land in just the right patterns. I am getting faster. I am getting better. Not so many patties are being burnt. Not so many hamburgers come out ruined.

I place cheese on the number that Keith specifies, and I leave them there long enough to melt. Then they are part of the batch I place on buns and slide to Keith. Faster, I think. I work faster, and better. I'm not Keith, but I am good. There is nothing in the world now but me and my work on the grill. No time to look around and see Sammy. My world consists only of twelves and twenty fours, and tens and twenties, of what is cheesed and what is not, of bottoms and crowns and the degree to which a bun is properly toasted. I cook as many as the grill will bear. Cheese thus and such, and a special order now and then. Trays of meat from the cooler. New trays of buns, ripping them free of the plastic that binds them. Sharpen the spat on the file. Wipe sweat from my brow. Grease drips from the filters in the ventilation hoods, drips to the grill, drips onto the burgers—now there is some secret sauce, I think—and with a few deft strokes I push the grease along so it runs down the gutters to the buckets underneath.

-4-

Shellaine has saved the day. With her quirt in hand she has trained her bear, and a trained and tamed bear is more acceptable here on High Hawk Road. The suburbs require a gentler bear. Burger Bear sings and dances as directed. The screaming has stopped. The noise is mostly giggles and squeals. The lines are steady, but not as mad, the lobby calm.

Kids push and shove to get close to Burger Bear. Mothers push, too. Shellaine suggests they take pictures of Burger Bear with babies in his arms, or sitting on his knee like Santa Claus. That is a hit. They want pictures. Come in tomorrow. Burger Bear will sit for you. She brings them back for a follow-up visit, another burger, more fries, a shake or two. Shellaine is a natural. They want free coupons, and she trains Burger Bear to be generous.

"Give the little boy a coupon for a free BurgerRoo," she says. Coupon redeemable next week. "Come back again."

Kids are everywhere, and more are coming. They hold Burger Bear's legs, pull his short tail, beg him to pick them up. Older children pull at him, at his head, his tail, his gloves, as if to expose his little fraud, but his outfit is made for abuse and the disguise holds. Some smart high school kids ask what is Burger Bear's sex, and how can you tell? Shellaine cuts them out of the herd, out of the store, off the lot, down the street, off to Box-A-Burger.

Burger Bear sings. His Lebanese songs are perfect, not of this world at all. They may have been in tune, or not, since Mideast melodies and chords are alien here on High Hawk Road. Burger Bear dances, picks up the darlings one at a time, dances around, carries them to the counter to order lunch.

"Burger Bear, Burger Bear, we love you…."

Shellaine invents the autograph. "Sign here," she says. Burger Bear dips his paw in ketchup, then presses it against a BurgerRoo box.

"Bears can't write," Shellaine says. "Bears have never been to school. Do you have any bears in your school?"

And the kids say 'No-o-o-o….,' long and slow.

With a snap of her quirt, Shellaine orders Burger Bear to tell stories. They take place in a land far away, near a desert full of genies and magic carpets. There are beautiful horses. And hamburgers, and cheeseburgers, in a land that has known no such delights. And French fries, flying everywhere, free to children. Then Shellaine herds the kids to the front of the store, sits them down quiet, and they eat. Burger Bear tells stories about how he chased genies that look like flies which come to steal hamburgers from the children in this far away place, of the Golden BurgerRoo that saved the starving town…

"Where do Burger Bears come from?" someone asks.

"From a country far away called Lebanon," Burger Bear says. "This Burger Bear," he says, "came to this place in America to ride horses. But the horses are gone." He does not explain hoof and mouth disease to the kids. "A great evil caliph threw them out of Persia."

"What's a caliph?"

Whack! goes the quirt. It is time to quiet the bear.

-5-

"God in heaven, what is going on here?"

Wackhoff comes in the back door. Tall, thin Wackhoff, as usual in a closely tailored suit, this one light gray, a crisp white shirt, laundered and pressed, his thin and wispy hair brushed over his head. His thin hair does not conceal the shiny strip that runs from his forehead to the rear of his skull. I nod. It is straight up noon, lunch time, crunch time, and the back line is a mess. Not even Keith will be able to save us. My half of the back line—the grill side of the back line—is a particular disaster. We are keeping the production up, the hamburgers fried, the French fries coming hot and salty, sandwiches wrapped and down the chute, but there are papers and meat all over the counters and on the floor, pieces of onions, pieces of pickles on the floor, stuck to the stainless, crisp dark fries floating in the grease, empty boxes tossed everywhere, and a dark patina built up on the grill so the meat is slow to cook.

"That's not frying," Wackhoff says, looking over my shoulder. "That's baking."

Keith does not say anything at all.

"The lobby is packed with more kids than Christmas at church," Wackhoff says. "I had to park next door at the Lucky Plate. What's going on here?"

"It's Burger Bear day." Keith says. "We are the chosen store. But the chosen one got drunk." He nods towards Baptist who lies crumpled in a corner on the floor. Keith barely turns his head to talk. He is a machine on the window now, garnishing sandwiches and wrapping them as fast as I fry them up, then sending them flying down the chutes to the front line. "Roll up your sleeves. You're in time to save us."

"Hell of a day to be short handed," Wackhoff says. Wackhoff takes off his jacket, carefully brushes it, then hangs it on the back of the office door. He sees Baptist. "Is this Lazarus whom we must waken?" Wackhoff gently nudges Baptist with the toe of his narrow Italian shoe. "Arise." Baptist does not move. "And if this be Lazarus, who is Burger Bear?"

"Sammy," Keith says. "My grillman."

A counter girl out front calls back a special order. "One wiener."

"Echo?" Keith says, turning to the window, asking her to repeat it.

"A wiener," she repeats. "I got a customer who wants a wiener."

"Coming up," Keith says. Then turning to me, "Gimme a puppy."

I toss a hot dog in the microwave.

"Lazarus, arise," Wackhoff says to Baptist, but without much conviction. "He was hell of a grillman in his day," Wackhoff says. "In his day. In his day. Lucky for him he owns so much stock. You know he owns a share of us. A little bit of every hamburger we sell is his. I can't fire his ass, you know, but he can fire me. That's how you know who's boss."

"We needed his ass today, however much stock he's got in the company," Keith says.

"Never a better grillman than ol' Richard Baptist. He could do the front line and the back by himself, and not have five minutes worth of mess to clean up, not even after the biggest rush. Did I ever tell you the time he ran the back line in the store down by the old Stadium." Wackhoff carefully adjusts his tie, burying it in his shirt, and rolling up the long sleeves. "It was night, you know, and I was night manager then. I had let the staff go that evening, things were so slow. We were down to the two of us, him and me. I was only staying open because there was a game that night and sometimes we got some business when the game got out. A football game. You know what the stupid son-of-a-bitches did at the game? Half time, we're down by twenty-eight points. So old man McKnowlton, Mr. Interburger himself, says the store is open and if our boys win—now they are down by twenty eight points—if our boys win, then its two-for-one after the game. Two-for-one! Bad enough, half price, but two-for-one doubles the fucking work. And our guys won. Second half, our boys score four touchdowns and a field goal. Who would a thunk it? Well, I had sent the whole staff home because night business down at the Stadium store was for shit, game or no game, but that night—like they came just to piss us off, the whole goddamned high school and their parents, and their dogs, from both sides, all went to Interburger. Hundreds and hundreds of them wanting their two-fers."

Wackhoff's tie is silk and he seems to stroke it. The clean aprons are in a drawer by Keith's desk. He sorts through them calmly, looking for something appropriate to wear.

"So, what happened?" Keith asks. He is wrapping, and I am cooking. I am nervous. I hate it when management looks over my shoulder.

"There were just the two of us in the store, I the night manager and old Baptist on the back line," Wackhoff says. "But we were great. And Baptist, he was, perhaps, the greatest grillman ever." Wackhoff touches Baptist's bare foot with the pointed toe of his shining black shoe. "We set a record for the most money ever in one store in one day, and we did most of it in two hours. And at two sandwiches for the price of one. Sold out, we did. Sold out of absolutely everything. Fries, shakes, cheese, meat, everything. At the end we were selling cheese sandwiches. Two for one. When the store finally closed, we did not have one paper cup in the store. And we did it by ourselves. We were everywhere, the both of us, flying around that store. Now look at him. A worthless tit." Wackhoff kicks his foot again.

Wackhoff has searched through the aprons, not looking for one that fit—they are all the same size—but for one that looks good on him. He wraps it around and ties it in back.

"Now, where do we begin," he says. He is not talking to me, nor to Keith, but to himself, looking over the back line and taking charge. It is not his store, but one of the many he supervises.

Baptist feels the kick on his foot. He gets up and crawls to the doorway. His head sticks out of the office door and he peers around the jamb. He walks on all fours. In his white shorts, his spaghetti straps undershirt, his thin bones look thinner, like a cat that has been shaved, or a rabbit skinned. His hair is a mess and he stares at us, then plops back and sits on his butt, his head propped up between his elbows which rests on his knees.

"Screw him," Keith says. He fires sandwiches down the trays on the steam table with a deliberate, well aimed flip of his fingers. "I have a new Burger Bear. A great Burger Bear. Take a look." He nods out front through the steam window. Wackhoff takes a quick look and after a few moments of following Sammy, nods and goes around to watch more closely.

The timer on the microwave rings out. I put the hot dog in a bun and them both in a paper boat and slide it along the counter to Keith who flicks it down the chute. "Puppy up," he says to the girls out front.

Wackhoff looks through the steam window again as if he cannot believe it. "Who's the trainer?" he asks.

"The trainer?" Keith asks.

"That little lady in the orange out there," Wackhoff says. "Is that our Shellaine?"

"Indeed," Keith says. He is proud. These are his creations. "She's great."

"An angel," Wackhoff repeats.

Shellaine is no angel. She has solid good looks, and she has a sense of independence about her, as if none of this means much to her. She works because she needs money. Her father has left the family, and while her mother has been searching for another man for the last ten years, Shellaine has come to depend on no one. She works hard. She is good at whatever she does. She now has Burger Bear standing on a small table in the lobby, and she lashes the table top with her stick. Burger Bear dances, and claps his hands and sings.

"An angel," Wackhoff repeats again. "Now," he says, and his whole mood shifts. "We need to get things squared away back here." It does not take Wackhoff long to figure out the problems. My grill is full of over-cooked meat, cheese which has melted and is running onto the grill, and buns which are burning.

"I think, my friend," Wackhoff says. "You need to be saved."

I do not deny I need help.

"A hat," he says. He stands beside me, surveying the grill like a surgeon inspecting a patient on the table.

"A hat?" I say.

"A hat." He points at his head, but he is looking at the tools beside the grill. He picks up a spatula and tests its sharpness. As he inspects his tools, he edges me out of my position. I give him my spat and fetch him his hat. He takes both without looking at me. He is surveying my work on the grill. He is shaking his head.

"Hey, Keith," Mary Lee says, peering through the steam table. "Someone out here wants a Big Mac."

"A Big Mac?" Keith asks. "Where the hell does he think he is?"

"He says he wants a Big Mac." She nods and smiles and shrugs her shoulders.

"He gets a Big Mac, coming up." Keith takes a BurgerRoo out of its box, squirts a little Thousand Island dressing on it and rewraps in white paper. ""Pick up on a Big Mac, echo," he yells.

"Big Mac pick up," Mary Lee repeats.

"Asshole," Keith says under his breath. But he looks at Wackhoff and smiles. "God bless them," he says. "Every one."

Wackhoff places the paper hat on his head carefully, centering it, making sure it does not muss up the careful flip of stringy hair that covers his bald spot. Then, as is the company policy, he tilts it jauntily to one side as is so carefully prescribed in the book of the way things are and will be done at Interburger. There is suddenly no place for me at the grill.

"Now, Chris," Wackhoff says, calmly. "Be so kind as to get us another tray of meat. Keith, get your ass in gear. Let's get the production going. Let's get that build up, okay. Blessed are the children for they shall be filled."

Then he begins. The spat goes down the row of meat, cutting the patties from the grill, and the Wackhoff flips them in what seems one effortless move. They land on their raw sides in a cleaner, more orderly pattern than I have put them down. With both hands, then, Wackhoff picks up the bottom halves of the buns, his fingers barely touching the grill as he pulls them off by the handfuls and deals them out on trays. Then, with another sweep of the spat, the meat leaps from the grill to the buns, and he picks up and deals out the crowns beside them, ready to be garnished and then finally constructed. "Blessed are the mothers of little children," he says, "for their children shall be happy. Blessed are those who make the burgers, for they shall be paid."

Wackhoff is flipping, and cleaning the grill with even greater speed and greater skill. In his hands it appears effortless. He barely moves, but uses every move twice, both coming and going. When he pushes something out, he pulls something back. As he adds to the mess I have made, he also moves to clean things up. The dark greasy build-up on the grill is cut away with each new rotation of meat and buns, and, as it is so, the patties cook quicker, look better, each patty which comes off has a fine brown patina. Wackhoff wastes no movements, leaves no space unused, misses nothing, makes no mess, and the trays slide down to Keith one after another in good time. Indeed, the meat obeys the many rules all the more because Wackhoff is there.

He does it all, and he has time to spare. He has time in between things that have to be done; extra time to do things like clean things up, time to wipe down the counter, to push the grease off the grill, to straighten up the cheese, to throw stray papers in the trash, to renew his spirit. Time to wipe his brow, to look around, to measure the flow and the tide, time to smile, time to manage. In minutes Wackhoff has brought order to the back line. I am amazed. I am impressed. Then, I realized I have fallen behind again. I have my work cut out for me to keep him going.

"Blessed are the restockers," Wackhoff is saying, looking at me. "For they will get their ass in gear and get the cheese." He smiles, but not a friendly smile. He knows he's good.

I restock the meat and cheese, bringing out fresh trays from the cooler. I rip open bags of buns, then take a turn or two on the fryers. But I watch him, my boss's boss. Wackhoff is a grill master, no doubt about it. He is better than me, better than Sammy, even better than Keith. The burgers sizzle in the places they are supposed to be, always in neat rows and columns, cooked to the right complexion of gray before he cuts them free and flips them to the other side to cook again. His meat is done, but it is still juicy, as it is supposed to be. He waves the shaker of salt across the grill like some artist with a brush giving his work a broad stroke of color. The patties are beautiful. The movements of his spat are beautiful. Everything that comes off his grill is perfect, the meat done, the cheese melted, the buns toasted warm and golden.

The spat in Wackhoff's right hand seems welded to his will. It goes where he desires. He uses it without looking, without thinking. Sometimes he has a spat in the left hand, too, and he works them together, chop, chop, chop, like a sushi chef. And he has that flair, as if he plays to an audience of more than me, but he is not playing to me. He is his only audience, and nothing seems to matter to him, but to please himself, as if who else is worthy to judge? Wackhoff doesn't sweat. He doesn't splatter grease on his shirt or pants. He smiles as he works. At times, almost under his breath, but still so I can hear it, he is singing.

Wackhoff works so fast even Keith is challenged to keep up, and soon Wackhoff is not only running the grill, but making the build, sidling down the counter to run the window as well, telling Keith what to do, and how to do it, when to move and what to wrap, where to stand, where they are falling behind, if only for a second or two. Keith gives way and does as he is told. Keith does it admiringly, easily. They are a team. Keith knows instinctively what he should do to support Wackhoff. He knows what Wackhoff wants, even before Wackhoff asks for it. They push and pull at each other, moving back and forth along the back line in harmony. Keith does what I had been doing—the fries, the buns, the cheese—only he does them better, faster, more in harmony. Wackhoff is on the window. Then back on the grill. He is everywhere.

And I am in the way. I am superficial here. No possible amount of work is enough for me to be needed. It is an enormous lunchtime rush. I see the customers out front, all our are registers open, customers line up behind them six, sometimes ten deep, and yet back here all is under control. I have nothing to do. Nothing important. I take out trash, sweep the floor, fetch meat, fetch buns, keep these two priests of fast food working at their furious paces. I help with the fries, I help with special orders, and, when a girl out front needs change, I run up front with a roll of dimes or quarters. Things nice to have done, but unnecessary to the great unfolding.

I am a mere ornament. A pimple on my master's butt.

-6-

"That's it, that's it," Wackhoff says. "Hallelujah! Who could have done any better?" Wackhoff tosses his spat into a slit on the grill where it resides like a pistol in a holster. He takes off his apron as carefully as he has put it on, folding it neatly so it can be reused. It is spotless—no stains, no grease, no streaks of blood. It looks as clean and fresh as when he has taken it from the laundry drawer ninety minutes earlier. He puts the apron on Keith's desk.

"Now," Wackhoff says, turning to Keith, "we need to talk. And I've worked up quite an appetite. The Lucky Plate?"

The Lucky Plate is the family restaurant next door. Wackhoff washes his hands at the sink, slow and sensuous from the palms to the elbow. He looks at his hands as he washes them.

"We'll leave this place to the B-team," Wackhoff says, nodding at me.

The rush is over. The lobby is quiet. Latecomers occasion in, but they come in numbers nothing like the earlier rush. Keith takes off his apron and wipes down the stainless steel counter. It is a mess, littered with buns and splotches of ketchup fired wildly from the ketchup gun, pieces of pickles and scattered bits of onion. The grill, however, is clean. Even after the busiest lunch hour I have ever witnessed, Wackhoff has left it spotless, his signature.

Keith is barely thirty, but he looks older. He is younger, in fact, than I by half a dozen years. His receding hairline ages him, as does his frown, and his thick moustache looks like a vegetable brush running across his upper lip. He is smiling and sucking on the ends of his moustache.

"First I'll do the hourlies," Keith says, but he has barely gotten the words out when Mary Lee comes around the corner with the cash register tapes. She is smiling.

"You're gonna like this," she says.

Keith just smiles. "You guys did good out there, Mary Lee. Get the girls on their breaks, and get the front cleaned up." But he is interested in the tapes, adding them up in his head as he walks back to his office. "Yes," Keith says. "This is good. Real good. " Wackhoff follows close behind, and they close the door when they are in Keith's office.

Baptist sits half in the store, half out the rear doorway. His body keeps the door from shutting. His eyes follow whoever walks by or steps over him. From time to time he tries to get up, but he can't. He wears only his white shorts and an undershirt. Now, as the warm light of the full sun creeps up to him, he turns on all fours and makes his way outside. He stops, then turns back.

"Tell them...," he begins. "Well, tell them I've gone." With that he turns and makes his way on all fours towards the parking lot and his bus. The back door swings shut on its pneumatic hinge, then shuts with a click.

Out front a kid is pounding on the bathroom door. "Let me in. Let me in. I got to pee pee."

Sammy emerges, and the kid screams at the sight. Sammy has been in the bathroom for some time, and he comes out carrying Burger Bear's head.

"You want me to cook now, Mr. Mann," Sammy says. His voice is quiet, plaintive. Sammy's hair is wet and plastered to his face as if it were greased down. Except for his head, he remains Burger Bear.

"Get dressed, Sammy," I say.

He stands waiting for a moment, looking at me. I lean back against the counter, staring out through the steam table window, wrapping sandwiches and cooking. "How did I do, Mr. Mann?" Sammy finally asks.

"You did well, Sammy," I say. "You were the best Burger Bear ever," I add. It is true.

He has been waiting for that. His eyes light up. "You think?" he says, childish and needy.

"You did fine, Sammy," I say. "Just fine. A lot better than Baptist." He has done well. I admit I feel jealous. I could have done it, but Sammy has the history now. Both Keith and Wackhoff have been impressed.

"Sammy!" Shellaine shouts. "You were great!" Shellaine comes around the other end of the counter to the back. "You were great! I'll work with you anytime." She is exuberant, and wears a catty smile, seductive, as if she and Sammy now have an understanding. "Keith must be pleased."

"You think?" Sammy asks.

Shellaine likes doing everything—working out front, cleaning and closing, working at the counter days, working nights, wrapping sandwiches and working the window, cooking fries and counting money, but most of all she loves working the grill. She gravitates there naturally. She fries until someone makes her stop.

"I'm sure everyone liked you, Sammy," I say, but he is looking to Shellaine and she looks up from the grill with that smile. With her spat in hand, she stops cooking for a moment, wipes her hands on her apron and goes to Burger Bear and hugs him.

"You were great," she says. "You were one of the great Bears."

"I am?" He believes her. Sammy relaxes.

"Sammy," Wackhoff says. He and Keith come out of his office. Wackhoff has his suit jacket on. Keith wears his baseball cap. "Sammy...." Wackhoff is beaming. He starts to hug Sammy, but when he is close he simply makes do by grabbing one of the big Burger Bear paws. "You were excellent. You were superior. You were...." Then after a moment's loss for words, he finds what he wants to say. "You were my dream of Burger Bear. The job is yours forever more."

"You were good," I repeat, maybe louder this time, but Sammy does not hear me. He smiles and looks down, his head seeming to contract inside the costume. He says nothing, as if whatever he says might ruin the moment.

Keith leads Wackhoff out the door. "Tomorrow," he says to Sammy. "We've scheduled Burger Bear tomorrow, and you're it. But for god's sake, get that uniform cleaned. It smells. Shellaine, you, too. A great team."

Tomorrow is Saturday, Sammy's day off, but he does not say a word. Keith leads Wackhoff outside and the two of them disappear into the bright afternoon. The door swings shut with a comforting thunk and click.

"Burger Bear is dead," I say. "Long live Burger Bear."

Afternoon

- I -

Shellaine cooks. Sammy is somewhere changing out of his costume. The lunch rush is over. Keith is next door at the Lucky Plate having lunch with Wackhoff. Mary Lee is on break, sitting in the lobby. I am listless.

"You working this afternoon?" I ask Shellaine.

"You want me to?" she says. Shellaine is exact and precise at the grill. Most men—Wackhoff, Keith, myself—push things along. Anyone watching would think quick and fast are virtues. But Shellaine is precise. She is steady. She is as productive as any man, grilling in a different way, more an artist, so full of grace that quick and fast are worthless.

I am in love with Shellaine. That is obvious. No doubt it is obvious to Shellaine. She is too young, of course, for me to be anything but a silent admirer. I am not a night manager who runs after counter-girls. But I am infatuated with her. I suspect it is a form of worship. It is as if I were her ghost.

"Sure, I guess," I say. "I don't know. Didn't Keith say?"

"He didn't say nothing. And anyway you're in charge. What do you say?"

"I want you to work tonight."

"I'll work now and tonight, too."

"You're too young to work all these hours, Shellaine."

"I can do it."

"I know you can do it. I just don't think you should."

"I can do it," she repeats. Then, taking that for an affirmative, she turns to the grill and keeps cooking.

Shellaine is not pretty. She is short, muscled, and her complexion is dark, as could be expected from someone half American Indian. But she is not native, or natural, or untamed. Still, I am fascinated by her hair, thick and black and as rich as some deep forest, braided in the back, one thick long braid that falls halfway down her back. She wears her brown and orange uniform well, but casual, tomboyish. She fills it out, but not in a seductive way. She is solid, and firm, and intense.

Her only other passion is long distance running which she does when high school is in session—she will be a senior next year. She runs cross country and has placed high in many meets. She runs the course, then keeps running, sometimes not even stopping to collect her ribbons and medals. She runs on. She runs away. She runs to work. Her mind runs. Work and running are all she cares about.

"Maybe you should clock out now, then come back tonight."

"I can stay. No problem." She is cooking. She does not look up from the grill. "I can do it fine."

"Why don't you clock out for a while, go run," I say. "It will do you good. I need Sammy to cook."

"Sammy's Burger Bear. Burger Bear doesn't cook."

"Burger Bear can get real for a little while. Go get your money. Let's close out your register."

I ask a girl from the front line, come back to run the grill, another to run the window. Shellaine brings her cash drawer to the office, then drops it on the desk. "You want me to count it out?" she says. The money is in the cash drawer with her register tape on top.

"I'll do it," I say. "I have to do something since I make the big bucks." I laugh. When she does it, she is faster and more accurate than I am. But it is my job for the moment.

I dump out her change. The idea is to leave fifty dollars in the drawer. All the rest should amount to the total on the tape. If a girl is short, we charge them. If they are over, we consider those errors as well. Interburger discourages anything but being exact. Keith likes things just so.

"You impressed the big guy," I say. She sits on the chair by the desk and watches me count out her money, catching me as I make small mistakes.

"I did?"

"You did," I say. "You and Sammy. Burger Bear and the Bear Master. You were a good team."

Shellaine is unimpressed. She corrects a pile of pennies that I have miscounted.

"I like working with Sammy. He's funny."

"I'd hate to lose you guys to the road. Keith would be devastated."

"What road?"

"The circuit. The stores. We got sixty stores. Burger Bear goes to all of them. Hit the road, as they say. Baptist is a drunk. You guys are better. Wackhoff says so. I'm sure you are part of a team."

I notice jealousy in my voice.

"I wouldn't like that," she says in a schoolgirl way.

"You don't want to travel the Interburger circuit?" I tease her, but I want her to say again and again she doesn't want to leave the High Hawk store. I want her to say she wants to stay and work with me. I want her to say I have more to teach her, she has more to learn, about work and life, how a good store ought to be run, how there are other minds inside other heads, what constitutes a poem, how often love comes as a surprise. I want her to say she likes me, to say she thinks I am funny. I want her to say she thinks I am as funny as Sammy. I want her to say I would make a good Burger Bear. Now there is a team, I think, Shellaine and I…. I wish she would say something.

"Bull," she says. She is counting the money again absently. She cannot help herself but work. "I hate travel. And that Burger Bear bit, that would get old. I can do it a couple of times. It is fun, with the kids and all. And Sammy. But anyway, where would that get you, being like a trainer for a fake bear? I mean, I couldn't even be the bear. I mean, is that a future or what?"

"Yeah?" It is a question, but I mean to draw out her reasons. What does Shellaine think. I want to know. She says nothing. She is not going to explain herself. I can tell. We will banter back and forth, and I will yearn to know her, be a sculptor, chiselling on her stone, taking all my skill to get beneath the surface of things, but never getting below.

"It's stupid," she says.

"Yeah?" I have finished my calculations and her drawer comes up five dollars short. I work the calculations again, recount the money, and she is still short. Shellaine looks at my tabulations, makes a correction and the amount comes out perfect.

"If I wanted to be stupid, I would be a manager," she says.

I look at her, then laugh. "Me, too," I say. I put her cash drawer in the safe. "If I am looking for a way to be stupid."

"Who knows?" she says. "Whatever is going on with Keith, who knows?"

"What's going on with Keith?"

"Over there," she says, shrugging in the direction of the Lucky Plate.

"What's going on over there?" I ask. "Do you know something?"

"Keith's not going to be around much longer. Things are going to change."

It is not a big smile, but it is a smile. Her lips never part, subtle, but seductive. They remain closed, and her sly smile wins me every time.

"What do you know? You know something."

"Nothing." But she knows something. It puzzles me how she always knows, but she does.

"Is Keith in trouble, or something?"

"I didn't say that." Her eyes are dark, like onyx, but there is no getting beyond the surface.

"You think he's out of here?" I am afraid to ask too hard, to show how much I relish the thought of Keith being fired. How I would rejoice.

"I don't know for sure," she says. "Nobody knows for sure, do they? I shouldn't've said anything."

"I had a dream last night...." I begin. I roll my chair back and look around the corner. From a certain place in the office, I can see out the door, around the equipment and stainless steel, along the back line and up through the last bit of window. From there I glimpse a piece of the Lucky Plate, that particular spot against a window where Keith and Wackhoff now sit having lunch. From there they can also see us, look down, keep an eye on things. I hesitate to tell Shellaine about my dream, but I want to.

"Keith leaving, I had a dream last night," I say. "The boss was dead. He fell on the grill and was fried to death."

"Oh," she says, but she is not upset. "I don't think he plans on anything like that."

"It is a recurring dream."

"I don't think he is planning to die," she says. She plays with a stack of pennies.

I often dream of Keith's death. Sometimes he dies. Sometimes I kill him. It is always a horrible experience for him. I never fail to enjoy it.

"But if he's gone," it occurs to me, "Interburger will need someone to run High Hawk Road. They will need a new boss. Who will they get, do you think?" Then I see where my logic is taking me. "It might be me."

I am not asking Shellaine, but I turn to her, expecting to hear an echo of what I am thinking. She doesn't say anything.

"What about that?" I suggest. "If I become manager, you can be night manager."

She smiles, shrugs her shoulders, and says nothing.

"Maybe you'll be manager," I say. I smile. Shellaine is smiling, too, but that tells me nothing.

"Who knows?" she says.

"Who knows?" I say. "We could be a good team."

"I could do it." She has a pigheadedness to her, an obstinacy, I think. I've never had such confidence.

"I'm sure," I say. I did not mean to offend her. "You could do the job. But you're young. You'd have to be night manager first. Be trained, you know? And finish high school, for god's sake."

Suddenly I worry. If Keith is leaving, or being fired. I should know. Maybe Wackhoff is firing him now. I peek at them through the window.

But that is how it is done. A supervisor shows up one day unexpectedly, and says, 'Let's go have lunch,' and then at lunch—out of the office, away from the help, away from the desk and from the safe, and the money, and the files, — 'You're fired, go away, don't come back.'

Then, more serious. "Are they looking for a manager? Have you heard something? This would be sudden."

"It is," Shellaine says. "But not that sudden. I thought you knew." She is absently spinning coins on my desk. They spin, then waver, then fall. Every time.

"Are you sure?" I ask. Nothing changes in her expression. "I wonder if they are talking about me."

I want her say something, I want her to say I am a natural candidate for the job, that I am a good manager, that I am the best and obvious choice, that she wants to be my night manager, that we will work together and turn this place around. I am thinking of how I will do that.

"Like I say," Shellaine says. "If I wanted to be stupid I'd go for it myself. Be a manager. Only I don't see myself as being quite that stupid yet. I'm still young."

-2-

I keep my eye on Keith and Wackhoff. The Lucky Plate is just across the ravine from Interburger, and I can see them sitting in the window and talking. Wackhoff talks. Wackhoff swings his hands about, like a chicken trying to fly. Keith sits and smiles and nods, his hands folded in front of him on the table.

Talking, talking, talking, Wackhoff waves his hands. Keith sips coffee and listens. Wackhoff swats at his own words like flies. When he laughs, Keith laughs. When he says something serious and points his finger at Keith, Keith looks back serious and sips his coffee. I am glad they are where I can see them. That seems important. I am glad they can see me at work, see I have things under control down here, that I keep a lid on the place. I can do this job, days as well as nights.

Keith leaving. I think of nothing else. Keith being fired. It is pleasant to contemplate. I wish it could happen. I would not dread coming to work. No one will be here to tell me what I have done wrong. I would be the boss.

There is no better candidate.

-3-

"What happened to Sammy?" I ask. It is almost two o'clock. I have been in the office counting out the registers. The counter girls have all gone except Mary Lee who always remains on the clock until five. Shellaine is on the grill, carefully cooking three or four hamburgers at a time, cleaning things up, putting things away, wiping down the stainless steel.

"Sammy's changing," Shellaine says. She bobs her head towards the restroom around the end of the counter.

"He's not dressed? It's two o'clock."

"He's cleaning his costume. It stinks."

"You can't clean out a bear costume in our bathroom!"

"No one told Sammy that."

Just then Sammy comes around the corner, barefoot and naked except for his boxer shorts, and dripping wet. He is huge and his dark skin hangs loose. He carries his sweatpants and his grillman's shirt.

"Sammy," I say. "For god's sake, you can't walk around half naked."

"There's no one out there," he says, nodding towards the lobby.

"I'm here!" I say. "Mary Lee is out there. And Shellaine…."

Sammy shrugs. He looks puzzled. "She didn't look." he says, nodding towards the front.

"That doesn't mean you're not naked."

"I'm not naked," he says. He looks truly puzzled. "I got shorts on. And sandals."

"Get dressed," I say. Sammy is dripping and leaves a wet trail. I wonder how he has washed in that tiny rest room, how he has cleaned up that filthy bear costume, and what sort of mess he must have left.

Later he emerges properly dressed, wearing his uniform—brown sweat pants and a brown polyester shirt with the Interburger embossed on the pocket. He is even wearing his paper hat, though Sammy hates it and never wears it unless he is told.

Without a word to me, Sammy starts his afternoon chores, first filtering the hot grease in the deep-fry fryers. He will run the grease through a contraption that separates out food particles from the grease, and then recycles the grease back into the fryers. Grease cooks food by sealing the outside of the food, and turning the moisture inside into steam. Good grease quickly seals food and leaves it crisp. Old grease cooks more slowly, seeps inside, making limp, soggy French fries that are dark. Fresh grease is transparent like water. Old grease is murky brown and foams when it cooks.

The filtrating machine is a pump on wheels. Sammy opens a petcock on the fryers and hot grease rushes into the tub. When he turns on the pump, it draws grease through the filter and back into the fryers through a hose and nozzle that is the same as a gasoline pump. He is whistling the Burger Bear Song.

"Hey, Mr. Mann," Sammy says. "What'd ya think? New grease today, or what?" Sammy is comfortable at work. He is quick at filtrating, and rarely spills a drop. The metal hose, the nozzle, the machine, all are like toys in his big hands and he has no fear of hot grease, none at all, even though he only wears sandals.

"You seem hoarse today, Burger Bear," I say.

"Too much singing," he says.

"I bet."

"I like the little kids," he says. "I like dancing."

"Do you like it when they bite you?"

"Ah," he says. "Burger Bear, BurgerRoo. New grease or do we give 'em the old for a few more days?"

I like being in charge. "What do you think, Sammy? You think we ought to change it?" That is the way I do things. I ask employees their opinions. Keith tells people what to do.

Sammy has a puzzled look on his face. "Yes or no, Mr. Mann?"

"What would you do," I ask, "if you were in charge?"

He looks at me, then he looks back at the grease, then back up at me. "If I am in charge?" he asks.

"Yeah. What would you do?"

"I'd take a nap," he says.

The point of being night manager is to be a manager some day. As a night manager, I have simply survived a period of training, gone to work, stayed until midnight, closed the store, gone home, got up in the morning, gone to work, trained to be a manager, did my duty, waited my turn. When I took the job, I thought my days would be my own at least. I could write poetry, or read, and go to cafes in the afternoon and sit outside sipping coffee in the morning, then go to work at night. But the job has turned out to be such a grind, physically and mentally, that I am chronically tired, too tired to go out to the cafes in the morning, sit on the sidewalks, write poetry, or even read. And when I come home at night, I am too tired to do anything but flick on the television and fall asleep in the gray light of the tube. I have lost my inspiration and my appetite. All that is left is to be the manager.

There have been openings at Interburger. In a chain like ours there are always openings, but for the first year I wasn't ready, and for the second year I have come to be convinced that Keith is not recommending me. I suspect that he prefers to keep me at High Hawk Road, that he prefers to have me rather than train someone new, that he likes having someone around whose ass he can chew, who comes to work days when he requires it, who runs the store well in the evenings, who puts up with his bullying. Me being there, I think, allows him to be nicer to everyone else.

Keith does not like me. That is obvious. He does not like the work I do, nor how I do it. But he never hates me enough to fire me.

And he needs me. Good night managers are hard to find. He might foist me off on another store, another manager, another supervisor, at Interburger, but I know him. He will want to create me first, make me perfect, like the perfect BurgerRoo, before he lets me out of his domain. He will want to say to his colleagues, 'There goes another one of mine. A fuck up that I tore down and rebuilt.' He has that military mind. But he will not get to me. I put up with him, but I will not let him get to me. I will not let him destroy me, and I will have his job. I am good in my own way. And I have been patient.

The filtrator is cycling the grease while Sammy waits for me to make a decision. He says nothing. He looks at me and waits. He bobs his head a bit, as if he is singing to himself. The Burger Bear song, I think. When I look him in the eye, he shrugs his shoulders.

"Let's change the grease," I say. "Let's give the crowd tonight some French fries to write home about."

"Okay," he says. "But the grease barrels are full out back. The truck's been broken down and just got fixed. Can we please leave the grease in the buckets if we come early tonight to pick it up?"

"Okay, leave the grease. Keith'd be on my ass if we left the grease bucket full."

"Oh, Keith don't mind. He knows the truck been broken. It's his truck."

"What truck's been broken, Sammy?" I ask. "You don't have a truck."

"The grease truck," he says. "The one we got to haul the grease in."

I don't say anything for a few moments. What Sammy is saying doesn't make any sense, but he seems to think I understand him clearly.

"That old man with that smelly truck picks up the grease out back." We sell him the grease for little or nothing, but are happy to get rid of it, to keep from going down the sewer and clogging it up. He in turn sells it downtown to a rendering plant that renders it back down to its purer parts. He gets gets grease for next to free, and is paid when he sells it. "A perfect racket, if you can put up with the smell."

"No," Sammy says. "Keith fired him. We do it now. My brother and I. For Keith. Keith got lots of customers. Too many for one little truck, that's for sure. That's what I tell him. We can't do all those places, I say. How long's the night? Keith calls me his grease monkey."

I am staring out the window above the steam table, wrapping the few sandwiches that are coming off the grill. Out front Mary Lee is badgering an old couple who cannot make up their minds what to order. It is the typical slow Friday afternoon on High Hawk Road.

I know nothing about what Sammy is saying. But it is obvious that something secret has been going on.

"Keith has you pick up grease?"

"I thought you knew," Sammy says.

"He's got a business on the side?" I am interested now. Managers should not have businesses outside Interburger. Interburger is supposed to be their life. All of it. They take vows to that effect.

"I thought you had to know. Keith'll kill me."

"How long has this been going on?"

"You better ask Keith. I don't think I better say nothing. They're his customers."

"What customers?" I ask. "Who are they? If you have a truck, you must have a lot of customers."

The grease is hot as it rushes from the fryer to the filtrator, then back again. "You want new grease, Mr. Mann, or you want to leave this?"

"How many customers? Do you guys work every night? How come I don't know about this?"

"Many customers," Sammy says. The filtrator is pumping the dark grease back into the pots. "Keith's grease route goes all over." Sammy says. "You should see what we see, the stink we put up with. I do the work. But what people put in those barrels—dead animals, or something, or old hamburger or something. Only supposed to put the grease in there, and run-off from the grill. The guy at the rendering place says, 'Hey, I don't mind a few crispies in there, but what you people putting in those grease barrels these days?' I say, 'What you mean 'you people.' I don't put nothing in there,' I say. I don't know, some people," Sammy says. He shakes his head. He opens another petcock and hot grease drains out into the filtrator. "They must put things like old dead animals, skunks, or dead cats, or something in them, I don't know. Maybe someone did. One old barrel of old grease looks pretty much like any other, you know. And some of them, I don't know how long they left that stuff sit out there, but sometimes it's got foam on top that's all green. And the places you got to go. You don't want to know, Mr. Mann."

He assumes I do not want to know. But I listen. This business of the grease route is news. For years Interburger has sold the grease to a service, then some months ago there were reports that someone was stealing the grease from behind our store. Rumors were that it was happening at other stores, too. Managing that is all part of the manager's job. Not mine. But if Keith is the one who is stealing the grease, or even if he is the one buying it from Interburger, then he is breaking the law or breaking the company policy.

"Dipping his pen in company grease," I say.

"I'm just changing this grease," Sammy says.

"So you and your brother pick up the grease." This is very interesting. "Let's just leave this grease here. It's pretty old, but I don't see any reason to let Keith steal it, too."

"We don't steal it," Sammy says. "It's a route. Keith's got it set up. We pick up everybody's. The steak house down the street. Box-a-Burger." He turns the pump on. The hot grease flows up and back into the fryers and Sammy hoses it around to rinse it out. "I keep ours clean. Good grease. Locked up.

Not everybody does. Some stores, they sit a barrel out there. God knows what's in it."

"Restaurant grease," I say. "What a racket...."

"It's a job," Sammy says. He looks up at me. The hot grease is flowing from the nozzle and he smiles. "Keith says go here, go there, I go. He says, pick up this grease, pick up that, take here, that's what we do, my brother and I. I don't like it, working late and all, but that's what Keith wants, so we do it. It's money, you know what I mean?"

He wipes down the fry pots with paper towels. They look nice, but the grease is dark. I will change it tomorrow.

Mary Lee calls over the steam table. "Hey," she says. "We got customers out here. BurgerRoo. Get to cooking, you two." A few people are standing in front of her register. The build of sandwiches we keep has dwindled down to none at all.

I force a smile. "Coming right away, Mary Lee. Right away." Mary Lee is all work. She is the nail that keeps me attached to my work. I would rather write poetry—even at work, or recite all the poems that I have memorized. I lay down patties to cook and buns to toast. "So, Sammy?" I ask. "Keith fixed this up, for you to go around at night and pick up grease?"

"Me and my brother," Sammy says. "Out back here, out back there. Didn't you know about it?" he asks. He has finished filtrating. "I don't think I should've said anything."

"It's okay," I say. "You guys steal grease at night, and I'm the night manager, we're in this together. I won't get you in trouble."

He nods, glad to hear he hasn't given away some secret. But he has.

"I just wonder who your customers are," I continue. "How many nights you work."

"Two or three nights a week," Sammy says. "You got the Interburger downtown, you got the ones south, north. You got all the Box-a-Burger. Lots a Box-a-Burgers. A couple MacDonalds. Burger Kings. Dairy Queens up on highway. Man, Dairy Queens got the grease! Lucky Plate here. Lucky Plate in Raytown. Every night, four or five places, you know? Then we take the barrels downtown."

I look at him and nod. I don't know. But he thinks I do. I put cheese on the patties that need cheese, and scoop the meat into the buns, garnish them, wrap them, and push them down to the steam table.

"Pick up on Roo, Mary Lee," I say. Now I feel good. Now I have something on Keith.

"The steak places got the stinkingest grease. I tell Keith, their grease not worth shit, we got to go there? But he wants it all. He works it out."

"Works it out with who?" I ask.

"Oh, you know," Sammy says. "Night managers. Or sometimes no one. Sometimes there's grease that no one cares about. You go late to a place like that. You don't want to get caught, huh?"

I don't say anything. I don't shake my head or anything. I lean up against the stainless steel cooler. This is almost more now than I can put into my brain while I work. I wait for Sammy to go on.

"It's not bad work," Sammy continues. Once he starts, Sammy likes to talk. "We only got caught once. You do exactly what Keith says, no trouble. That's what I say. I don't mind work, not even wrestling a big old stinking barrel of grease around, me and my brother, in the middle of the night, out back of some rat hole when the rats are out—they're everywhere, you know. They go to the best places, the biggest rats. Steak places got the biggest rats. Always bones out back of a steak place. Plenty a bones. The rats don't eat the bones. The rats eat everything else—and leave the bones. But every place got rats. You think to yourself, now here's a nice place, there'd be no rats here, but they are there. We see them. Sometimes we have to wrestle the grease from them, that many wanting what they think is theirs. I told my brother, I'm glad those rats don't have a truck, there wouldn't be no grease left in this town."

"Are you guys cooking back there?" Mary Lee says. She is stretching as far as she can to look back into the steam table. "I got customers."

"I'm cooking, Mary Lee," I say. "I'm cooking." I throw fresh meat on the grill, a ten and an eight, then buns to match, but my attention is on Sammy. I fear that asking too many questions might make Sammy suspicious, that he will know I am ignorant of what he and Keith have been up to. It might or might not be illegal. It is most certainly against company policy. It gives me a sense of power to know.

"It's no good getting caught," Sammy says. "It wasn't my fault that time I was. We were at this one place, but they had a chain on their grease shed. We couldn't get in, so we went back the next night with cutters. The manager was waiting for us. Fired the night manager Keith was working with. Keith had to come down and get us out of jail. He talked them out of sending us back to Lebanon. But I don't mind a little trouble now and then, you know what I mean? We take it to a place across the state line. A guy dumps it in a vat and renders it down. I don't know what happens to it after that."

"Cleansing cream," I say. "There's a soap that's one quarter cleansing cream. Well, that's mostly old hamburger grease."

"No kidding," Sammy says. Finished with the filtrating, he turns on the pump and returns the grease to the last set of fryers. As they fill, he turns on the gas to reheat the grease. "Americans!" He shakes his head. "Old grease into beauty cream. I love this country."

"I do, too," I say. "I got him."

"You what?"

"Nothing," I say. "I love this country, too."

It has come together—the whole story on a day when I need to have something on Keith. Keith is stealing grease. Keith is breaking company rules. Sammy knows and now I know. And it seems clear that I know why Wackhoff is here today. He has come to talk to Keith about stealing grease. He has found out about Keith, just like I have. Perhaps the police have called him. Perhaps he has heard from his many friends in the restaurants in town. He has come here to fire Keith. Keith is dead.

It is perfectly clear.

This is the way they do it. Wackhoff comes at noon and checks out the place, saying nothing at all while he is in the store, but after the rush asks Keith, 'Why don't we go off a while and talk,' and they go to the Lucky Plate, 'It's close, and let's sit and eat,' and then Wackhoff starts, first waving his arms and not quitting until he is finished saying all he wants to say, until Keith, the boss, is dead.

This is how the big bosses do it, I think. No lie detector for the big bosses. Down here, for us, they bring in the little black suitcase, the wires, the questions, to make us sweat. Up there, the bosses take the bosses to a booth and spread out papers on a table, and maybe eat and maybe they don't, and maybe the big boss has a little glass of wine and the little boss has a beer, and maybe they have wires that go to their brains and their bodies, and they stir those papers, and they ask those questions, and they get to the truth. Down here, with us, they have the little suitcase, a man to turn some knobs on it, wires to the heart and the hands, a roll of paper and a fluctuating pen that makes some marks—all to determine what is true and what is not.

I see them again from the corner of the back line, around the front, out the window, up the hill, inside the window of the Lucky Plate. It is almost over. Gloriously over. The boss is dead.

I smile. Sammy looks up and smiles, too, but he has no idea why.

-4-

Interburger has its way of finding the truth. I have seen their methods. A few months ago I arrived at work a bit earlier than usual. It was winter and dark outside, even at four in the afternoon, and cold.

The store was not busy. There were occasional customers. The door to Keith's office was closed, and, without thinking, I opened it. There they were—Wackhoff sitting at Keith's desk, Keith standing to one side with his arms folded, and, sitting in a metal folding chair across the desk from Wackhoff, one of the new girls who worked the day shift. She wore her uniform, but wires ran from the box to her arms and fingers. Another wire was strapped around her waist. The box on Keith's desk looked like a small suitcase.

"Get out," Keith says, turning to me. He pointed me out the door, then quickly shut it behind me. I heard it lock.

They had been giving the girl a lie detector test. Wackhoff called the black box on the desk his lie detector machine. Wackhoff had been trained to use it, I am told, and it was his favorite tool. He used it whenever there was a problem with the girls, or with the night manager, or a grillman, or anyone. When Wackhoff interrogated someone, or if for some reason he came to doubt their honesty, or if he wanted to threaten them into confessing, he asked them to submit to a lie detector text. 'Don't submit,' he would say, 'that's fine, you're fired.' He knew how to work it, I am told. He used it to get at the truth.

It made me nervous. How would I react if I was wired to such a thing? Who doesn't have something to hide? I was told to expect questions like, 'Do you masturbate?' What should I say? No? and give them a baseline for my dishonesty. Or, be humiliated with the truth? Everyone sometime had taken a cheeseburger from the steam table and eaten it because they had rushed to work without lunch. Or, who hadn't had time to take a break, and thought thus that Interburger "owed" them a little something and took it. Or taken home a pencil? Or a paper hat to use on Halloween? I mean, here's the thing. Wackhoff is sitting there with all these wires hooked up to you, and he sees the paper traces on the machine and you can't. And he's got this suit on, nice lightweight Brooks Brothers maybe, or Hart, Schaeffer, Marx. You are sitting there in your little brown and orange uniform, if you work on the counter, brown shirt if you work on the back, and you must wear your little paper hat. You sit there, and Wackhoff looks you in the eyes and says, "Did you ever steal anything?" and if you say 'No,' then he knows you're lying and god knows what is going on with his machine, the dials, the needles. And if you say, 'Yes,' you're done, you've dug your own grave. So, what do you say? Do you get fired for lying or fired for telling the truth.

Here's the point—you're on the machine, you've made Wackhoff go to all that much trouble, and you're gone, one way or the other.

The girl in the office is guilty for sure. After I had stumbled into Keith's office while she is being questioned, I saw her only once again, when she came back to the store at night to return her uniform. I heard she did not even get much past the first two questions. She broke down and cried. Most do, I have been told. There is no way to resist that force. In the minds of those young kids there may be no greater force on this planet than Wackhoff's eyes and his confident, off-handed way of asking questions you do not want to answer. There is no greater fear than to hear his firm voice as his hands adjust the dials on his machine. The threat is there, and if that is not enough, there is the machine. Only he can see it, the dials, the lights, the needle. Only he knows the truth, no matter what the truth is, no matter what you say. Did you ever wet your bed? I think I did, but I'm not sure. Did the machine reflect what I think might be true, or does it know the truth for sure apart from what I remember? Should I confess to what I think the truth is because—if I only think I have sinned—have I sinned? I think so. That would be the truth in the machine. But they make you answer, yes or no. There is no measure for, "I'm not sure." There is no place for qualifying your answers—that I don't know if this has truly happened, or if I only dreamed it once or imagined it whole. He believes we all have wet our beds. This is the truth with which he calibrates his machine. This is how Wackhoff measures it. But I am so nervous now, sitting here, I haven't said a word, yet he knows that I am lying. Have you ever masturbated? Have you?

Always the tears. Even men cry, I hear told. I suspect I would cry. And then they quit their jobs. It's better that way. How can they stay if Wackhoff knows the truth? Wackhoff agrees. It's better if you quit, then we won't prosecute. No one has ever been charged with anything, despite all the threats to bring in cops. The machine, the procedures, are that good.

The lie detector. I'll tell you what I think. It's an empty box with wires. Wackhoff asks questions. He knows the truth. He needs no machine. But he makes it look that way, he makes it look as if he depends on the machine to tell him all. After all, everyone hides something and, if properly confronted, everyone will confess. It is not Wackhoff's skill at running some machine that is the danger. It is his quest for truth. Truth is his knife. We are butter. Tears will come, but tears are aftereffects to loss, and never to any avail. Not here. Then comes the resignation. That is what Wackhoff wants, after all. That is the dance of death. When he starts these little journeys, they all end only in the one place they can end. Turn in your uniform. We will not prosecute. And we will apply your last week's wages against the things that you have stolen and the trouble you have caused us.

She was day crew, that poor girl I saw entangled in that machine. I never got to know her, not her name, not even her face until that evening she came in to return her orange and brown uniform. It was clean and pressed, like new. She was crying. And then she was gone.

-5-

At three o'clock Mary Lee comes to the back line and says she wants to leave early. She has arranged for Shellaine to work in her place.

"I guess that's okay," I say. "Is Shellaine still here?"

"She's been sitting out front on the curb for an hour," Mary Lee says.

I say it's fine if she leaves early.

"Don't you have anything to do?" I ask Shellaine. I have gone outside to talk to her. I squat to my haunches. We sit in the shade of the store. It is a warm, sunny Friday afternoon. The sky is clear and deep blue. Shellaine still wears her uniform. "You hang around here too much."

"There's nothing else to do," she says.

The heat makes my head itch.

"What do kids do these days in the summertime?"

"Work."

"Not all the time."

"No."

"What else? What do your friends do?"

She doesn't look at me, but plays with a stick in the street. The shadow of the restaurant moves away from the sun. "Drink," she says. "And drive around," she adds, like that is the complete list.

"Nothing for fun?"

"Drink."

"You know what I mean."

She looks at me funny.

"I don't mean that. You know what I mean. Just, for fun."

"That's it—work, and drive around—that's why I hang out with Bryan. He's got a car. And we drink a little. When there's school, I run…." My night grillman Bryan is in love with Shellaine. He is tall, young, goofy, and awkward, and he wears his heart on his sleeve. Shellaine hangs around him because he drives her around. He has a car. He worships her.

"You could run in the summer. Get ready for track season." She is a long distance runner.

"They don't have track in the summer."

"You could just run."

She does not respond.

"Is that all kids do?"

Dreaminess comes to Shellaine's eyes when she thinks. "Some kids have parties. Some kids are having a swimming party."

"Yeah? That sounds like fun."

"Does it?" she says, looking at me, that faint smile on her face, which is either a sarcastic laugh, or innocence.

"Well," I say. "It sounds different."

"It's what the squirrels do," Shellaine says. She returns to scratching the shadows on the asphalt with her stick. "I don't know those kids anyway."

"So," I say. "That's youth today. Working, driving around, drinking, and from time to time, going for a swim."

"That's it," she says. "That's youth today."

It is warm outside, even in the shade. Where the sun strikes the asphalt, heat rises in wavy lines of air, shimmering up and making whatever is beyond seem insubstantial. Traffic is light on High Hawk Road. No cars turn into our lot. The hunger for BurgerRoos has ebbed.

"And running," I say.

"And running."

"Too hot to run today," I say.

She nods and moves her stick on the asphalt.

"Mary Lee wants to leave early. You want to clock in?"

She looks up at me. She is quite lovely. Shellaine's face is round and soft and young. She carries a sad innocence about her. Her hair is a long braid down her back. I will never understand her. I feel shut out, close to her, yet she is forever out of my reach.

"Why not?" she says.

She stands and brushes her pants clean in a way that would otherwise be provocative. With Shellaine there is no hope, and without hope there is no provocation.

-6-

"Oh, " Beth says when I call her on the phone. "It's you. I'm glad."

"Who else might it be?" I ask.

"Any one," Beth says. "Everyone seems to be calling me today. How are you doing?"

I had planned to call Beth earlier, but I had been thinking about Keith now that I knew he was stealing grease.

"Okay," I say. "Now that Keith's out of here for a while. He's such a jerk, don't you think." She does not respond, but she never does when I complain about Keith or anyone else at Interburger. She is loyal to this company in a way that I can never be. I cannot help but struggle; she cannot help but be kind. "Who's been calling you?"

"Oh, everyone," she says. "I'm in big demand."

"Me, too," I say. "Working a double."

"So I hear."

"You hear everything," I say.

"Almost."

"Last night..." I pause. I want to get this right. "I loved it. It was so.... it was something."

"It was something, alright," Beth says. She sounds sincere. "I enjoyed myself."

"It was something, yes," I say. Words are stupid, but I am relieved she repeats them. "Of course, I didn't get much sleep." I laugh a bit. "Not that I cared."

"You were sleeping pretty good when I left," she says. "I hear you overslept and were late for work."

"I didn't oversleep. They didn't call me until ten. I was in by ten thirty. I am fine except Baptist shows up drunk. Sammy had to be Burger Bear. I ran the grill."

"And Wackhoff. He really showed his stuff, I hear."

"Good thing he showed up. I don't think I am ready to run the grill for a big crowd. And Keith goes crazy. He's a madman. And he takes it all out on me. You do hear everything, don't you?"

"I get some news from time to time."

Beth knows everything. She finds out stuff quickly. I don't know how.

"Something's going on," I say. "Wackhoff's here. He's having lunch with Keith at the Lucky Plate."

"Do you know what they are talking about?"

"No." I tell her about the lunch rush, Baptist, Sammy and Wackhoff's mastery at the grill. "Keith doesn't confide in me."

"Something's going on."

"You don't know?"

"Not for sure."

"Wackhoff's been talking to Keith, waving his arms like he does."

"He always waves his arms. He waves his arms when he's happy. He waves his arms when he's mad. And when he's excited, and he's always excited."

"What do you mean, excited?" I ask "When did you see him excited?"

"Lots of times."

I am embarrassed at how jealous I feel.

"It's about grease," I continue. I pause to see if she will say anything, but she does not. "Keith's been stealing grease. I think Wackhoff's found out and Keith's being fired."

"Grease?" Beth says.

"I'm pretty sure," I say. I tell her about Sammy and the grease barrels, the truck and the other stores. "Sammy steals grease at night, going around, swapping full barrels for empty ones, then sells them across town."

She is silent. "How do you know?" Beth asks.

I am in heaven. I have scooped Beth on gossip. She is listening.

"Sammy told me."

"I don't know, Chris….."

"No, no," I say. "I know more. Keith sets it up. Keith owns the scam. Sammy works for him. Keith sells the grease, arranges kickbacks. I got him." I am convinced I am right. "I got him by the balls for sure."

Beth is beautiful, and Beth is nice. She also knows politics. For the moment she is quiet. "I wouldn't take that to Wackhoff," she says. "Not now. Think about it first."

"I don't have to think about it."

"Let's talk about it first," Beth says. "We need to talk anyway."

"Oh, anytime," I say. "But what I said about Keith is true. It's fine if you don't believe me. But the facts fit. The grease out back. Sammy's story. Little things I've heard around. But we'll see. We'll see."

As I think about it, I am more certain I know what has happened. Keith has created a company that scams Interburger out of its income from old grease. He is stealing, although in a sophisticated way. When I get the word to the right people, Keith is finished. His reign is over. He will not be around to terrorize me. I do not mind that Beth is quiet. That has been my dream. But her silence, her reluctance will not change my plans to nail Keith.

"Have you talked to Dandison recently?" Beth says. "I got a call today."

"Ed Dandison?" I ask. "Mr. Box-a-Burger?" He is my friend as well as hers. Dandison drinks too much, and he talks too much when he is drunk, and he is always talking.

"He called," she says, and she laughs a bit. "You won't believe what he wanted."

"Dandison," I say with disdain. I feel promoted to manager already. I feel I should defend Interburger. "Box-a-Burger," I snarl. "I want my own Interburger. He's always calling. He's always saying something."

"He offered me a job."

"Really?" That is odd, although Ed is always promising jobs. Box-a-Burger is expanding and hires anyone who will work. "A real job?" I ask. "Or one of Ed's pie-in-the-skies?"

"A real job," she says. "Managing a store. There's a new one opening across High Hawk Road."

"Congratulations," I say. "You take it?"

"No." She pauses. "I thought you might be interested. I told him to call you."

I laugh. The timing was crazy. A few hours ago I would have thought about it seriously, anything to get away from Keith, but now I know this store is mine. My future is here. Box-a-Burger is the competition.

"I'm glad you didn't take it," I say. "I know where my next job is. And I'd hate to be competing with you."

"We need to talk," she says.

"Sure," I say. I want that. I want her to be part of my life. I want us to talk. I want us to be a team someday, managing our own stores, supervising our own chain. She makes me feel good about things. She makes me forget about Keith. "Come over after work. You can help me close again."

"I'll come over, but I can't talk now."

I am not listening to her. I am thinking about the changes I will make to High Hawk Road, the way things will be.

"I got ideas," I say. "I want to run them by you."

-7-

Ed Dandison had been night manager at High Hawk Road until Wackhoff fired him, then hired me. Dandison found another job right away managing the Box-a-Burger a half mile down High Hawk Road.

I like Ed Dandison. He is a tall, thin guy, with long arms, and he is awkward and gangly when he moves. But after a few drinks by late afternoon he smooths out. His jaw moves in a circle as he talks, and he is always talking. He gets along well enough with the people who work for him, and he has kept in contact with his night crew who now work for me. He even called a few days after I started working his old job. He likes to gossip and give advice.

Dandison has worked a long time in the restaurant business and he knows everyone in Interburger. He spends hours on the phone circulating rumors and gossip, about jobs and new restaurants.

Dandison has blond hair—on his head, his arms, and his eyebrows. The hair on his head is unkempt, even now as it is thinning out and he is growing bald. A round spot on the back of his head makes him look like a Franciscan, but he brushes his remaining hair around that spot, reminding me of a flimsy bird's nest with a shiny spot in the center. His eyebrows are bushy and wild, and the same bushy hairs protrude from his nose. He is older than the rest of us, so old curly wire-like hairs grow out from his ears like brambles.

Dandison is nice enough. We get along. He knows me because he knows my job at High Hawk Road. He had it for eight years. The labor market was tight, I think, or Keith would have fired him long before. Still, when Wackhoff became the supervisor of the district, he brought in a new way of doing things. I was supposed to be part of that. Like Beth, I was part of the "new bunch." Dandison and a whole generation of night managers and grill men were fired. Dandison had spent too many years sitting on his butt in the back of the store, drinking all evening, and talking on the phone.

Dandison still drinks, but he works hard at Box-a-Burger and his store is strong competition. Box-a-Burger is an aggressive chain constantly opening new stores, and they always need new people, new managers, new staff. When Dandison calls me early in my shift, the first thing he asks is if I want a new job. He always keeps me in mind, he says, if I ever want to jump to Box-a-Burger. He does not care about me. He wants to steal me from Keith. He wants to steal anyone from Interburger. Now he has approached Beth. She talked with him. It makes me wonder about her.

Dandison always talks about Keith. Dandison is usually too drunk to remember what he says, and when we talk he invariably tells me the same stories, how he hates Keith and how Wackhoff fired him.

"I didn't get fired by any old asshole," Dandison says. "I got fired by the supervisor. Wackhoff called me up on his car phone when I am at work. He says he is on his way to the store and I am to meet him outside. I didn't know what the guy wanted, you know? But it's always bad news when a supervisor comes to your store. It scared me every time he walked in, sat down, ordered a burger. But what's a night manager to do?

"I did what he told me," Dandison continues. "I stepped outside, and Wackhoff came wheeling his little red convertible up the drive. The top was down. He pulled right up next to me. It's dark back there, as you damned well know, and it was darker than normal that night, standing in the shadows of the Burger Bear sign out front. He comes wheeling in, poking me with those bright lights, then he flips them off so it was as dark as an old stone well.

"Wackhoff," Dandison continues, "did not even get out of the car. He says, 'Give me the keys.'

"And I say, 'What keys?'

"And Wackhoff says, 'The store keys, and keys to the side door, and the keys to the safe, the night deposit box, all the store keys.'

"I didn't know what to do, so I handed him my whole key chain. All my keys were on it, to my house, my car, keys I didn't even know I had. I gave them all to Wackhoff.

"Then Wackhoff told me, 'You're fired.'

"I asked him, 'What for?'

"And Wackhoff said, 'Cause I said so, and that's enough.'

"Then I said, 'Well, that's not right, and that's not enough.'

"Then Wackhoff started in. He said what's right was what he said was right. And he said he knew things. He said one time I took home a case of cheese, which was true. I borrowed it. I brought back as much as I borrowed. I replaced every slice of it. And I still don't know how he knew. That happened a year before he fired me, so what's he do, keep these things on some list of some sort?

"'I don't care if you paid it back or not,' Wackhoff said to me. 'If you paid it back, you're a dumber shit than I thought, because you're fired whether you've paid us back or you still have the cheese. And you are an even dumber shit for telling me you did it, because before I might not a' been so sure. Now I know, and I am double sure you are too dumb a shit to be working for me. So you're fired.'

"Can you believe it? I said. 'Fire me, I don't care,' I tell him. 'But I'm no thief. There's nothing missing from this store.'

"'You take the lie detector test?' he asked.

"And I say then and there to him, 'That lie detector business is bull shit,' and Wackhoff said he knew it. He said he wanted to know if I would take it, because not taking it proves I'm lying. 'Not sure-fire proof,' he says. 'But enough for me.'

"Wackhoff went on. 'That counter girl you were fucking?' he says. 'That's against company policy.'

"How did he know about that, I wondered. Hey, I am involved with the little sweetheart. Hell, she chased me long enough. I never lied to him about it. I wanted it in my record that I tell the truth. 'Everybody does it,' I said. 'If there's something wrong with fooling around with counter girls, then you got problems with most managers you got working here.'

"Then Wackhoff said, 'You don't know that. You were fucking her last night.'

"'She needed to get a ride home,' I told him. 'She needed a ride to work, then she needed a ride home.'

"But then the little bitch must've told him. Wackhoff said, 'Then why'd you take her to your place?'

"'How'd you know I did that?' I asked him, but he didn't say a word. I thought he was going to ask me to take that lie detector test again, so I said, 'That's maybe true, maybe not, but that's none of your business. And so what?'

"But what I wonder, Chris, is how Wackhoff knew all this stuff? Who told this stuff to him? Did he ask people and they told him? Or does he sneak around and watch? Or was he guessing, and I let myself get caught?"

"Like Santa Claus," I say. "You better think twice."

I put up with Dandison and with hearing the same old story I have heard a dozen times because I want to hear what Dandison knows about Keith, Wackhoff and Interburger. I want in on any gossip. I do not hang up. He is drunk. I do not trust him when he is drunk. But I trust him more when he is drunk than when he is not.

I see them in my mind, Dandison in the dark of the store outback, and Wackhoff in this red convertible—in the shadows the red car is as dark as the shadows, the dashboard a panel of orange lights and the car rumbling softly. Dandison says Wackhoff never got out of the car, but sat there, the dashboard lit up like a space ship. I know the car. Wackhoff still drives it.

"Wackhoff said, 'See this?'" Dandison says. "Wackhoff was holding up this little thing no bigger than his little prick, white and hard to see there in the dark, in the shadow of the store, the headlights knifing across the back lot. Chalk, that's what he was holding up," Dandison says.

"'See this,' old Wackhoff tells me.

"'I see it,' I say to him.

"'I mark tires with this,' Dandison tells me. 'And when the marks are in the same place when you come in as when you go out, then I know you have stayed where you are supposed to stay. And our managers are supposed to stay in their stores. Not leave a bunch of kids to run them. And, you have been leaving the store when you should have been in it. I know. I marked your tires, so I know.'

"'When's that?' I ask him. Wackhoff pulls out this little book and starts reading off dates and times. No shit, dates and times. 'Thursday evening, such and such a time and such and such a time, chalk marks indicate car moved. Friday evening, such and such a time, night manager's car has moved.' I know then that Wackhoff knows everything about me, every mistake I have ever made, every thing he needed to know, all in that book. I'm no saint. I made mistakes. I'm good at what I do, but who's perfect? But I figured he is paying more to find out how to fire me then he ever paid to have me work here.

"I mean," Dandison says, "that car did move. I don't deny it. I loaned it to my girl friend, the counter girl I am fooling around with. Stupid little twit. She was always needing this or that, and never wanting to work, and wanting to go and come back, and every time she needed to borrow my car. So what was I to tell her? I mean, Wackhoff got it wrong, I never left the store those nights. She took my car. It was her that moved it. I am fucking her so I had to let her take it if she wanted to from time to time, or she would tell him I was fucking her. And he would fire me. But the truth was as bad as what he thought, you see. So he would have fired me just the same. And he does. Maybe she was the one who told him all this stuff. Maybe no matter what I did, she was going to tell. What I had done was what any red-blooded American boy would a done. But it's in the book you don't. So, you fuck the help, you are wrong. You don't fuck the help, what kind of guy are you?"

"No shit," I say.

"I mean, is this America, or what?"

"Kind-a like a Soviet Interburger," I say. "Maybe that's what they want to run here."

"No shit," he says. "I never stole a fucking nickel from this place."

"I'm sure not."

"Cheese."

"Yeah?"

"But not a nickle."

It was his drinking that got him fired. Maybe, drunk, he got the wrong person on the phone one night and talked too much, and though he never remembered it, it was the conversation that got him fired.

"He was cocksure," Dandison says. "That pissed me off the most, Wackhoff sitting there smug in that little red Saab, not even getting out of it to fire me. He didn't even turn his car off. He turned down the radio. I stood there a while. I'm not sure who was supposed to say something next. Finally I said, 'Can I go get my stuff?'

"'Fuck, no,' Wackhoff says. Loud and clear, like that. One word, then the next word, 'Fuck, no. You're fired. Fuck, no.' And I have worked there for eight years, same shit night manger job, got the place cleaned up, cause when I went there it was a dump, for sure. I trained his crews. All that time, not a bad word from Interburger, not one bad performance review, nada, then bang, 'You're fired, fuck, no.' You know what he said next?"

I say I don't know.

"He said I was a drunk, and I should get help. I looked at him, and I was so mad then I could see him, however dark it was. I looked at him hard, and I said to him, 'Fuck you.' That's exactly what I said, and I didn't mind getting fired if I could say that to him. 'Fuck you, then,' I said again, cause he was speechless. Speechless. Then I turned and walked off. I didn't say another word. I didn't ask another question. I turned and walked off towards my car. I was so mad. And I got to my car, and I reached in my pocket and I realized I had given that little prick my car keys. You know what I did?"

I say I don't.

"I walked off. I didn't look back or anything. I walked past his car and down the lot and out to the street, and I walked home. It took me an hour and a half, but I did it, I didn't say a word, I walked home."

The first time Dandison called me was only a few days after I started working his old job, two weeks after he was fired. He called me to tell me this whole life story for some reason, like I care, like I am interested. I am glad to hear about Keith and Wackhoff, so I put up with his drunken rambling. It is good to know stuff about people you work for.

I am glad he was fired. I am glad I got his job. And I am glad he was incompetent. That makes me look better.

But better than Dandison is not good enough for Keith, and never has been.

-7-

The boss is dead, or as good as dead. He is sitting at the Lucky Plate while Wackhoff chews his ass. Wackhoff must know about the grease. If I have found out, then Wackhoff must surely know. Wackhoff knows everything. If he spent time and money to find out if the night managers are fucking the help, he surely spends time and money to find out if the day managers are fucking with the grease.

Soon enough this would be my store.

Everywhere I turn, I see things I can do better. A new kind of pie, for instance—dessert increases revenue per customer. Pie is good. And our shake machine only makes two kinds of shakes—chocolate and vanilla. I once suggested to Keith we should improve on that, add flavors or vary them over the year, like a peppermint at Christmas, and something green and minty on St. Patrick's Day. Pumpkin for Thanksgiving. Keith looked at me like I was crazy. Months later, the big chains started adding flavors, changing them through the year. Pumpkin on Thanksgiving. Interburger could have scooped them. Instead we stayed with chocolate and vanilla.

I have other ideas. I should take them right to the top, right to Wackhoff.

"Sammy," I say. He is cleaning out the cooler. "I need some bananas."

Sammy looks at me funny. He is on his hands and knees wiping down the stainless steel walls. The compressors drone. The coolers have a damp metallic smell.

"Run out to the grocery store and get a bunch of ripe bananas. Not too dark. But not green. Just right. And a big can of chocolate syrup." I give him money. "And," I say, "find me some of those little sticks. Like what Popsicles are on."

"What's a Popsicle?"

Sammy is back in fifteen minutes. "What's this for?" he asks. "We don't make nothing out of bananas."

"Sammy, my friend," I say. "This is gold. This is a moment to tell your grandchildren. This afternoon we are creating a new food. Can you keep a secret?"

He looks at me wide-eyed, like a child. "Sure," he says.

"The Chocobonono," I say. "Soon the world's new confectionery delight. What do you think of that?"

It is revolutionary. The name itself will sell it. It came to me in a flash one afternoon a few months back. I had had a sugar craving, a yearning for chocolate, yet I was telling myself I should eat more fruit. Too many hamburgers. Too much grease. A banana. Frozen. Dipped in chocolate. The Chocobonono. A frozen, quick-dipped, chocolate covered banana on a stick.

I made it. I experimented at home and in the evenings at the store for a month. It tasted good. The chocolate has to be sweet, and it has to be thick so it will freeze. The banana has to be a certain ripeness, no more, no less. The syrup has to be hot, very hot, and then the banana is dipped quick, then cooled, then dipped again and cooled, and again. Then quick frozen, or the banana might turn colors.

I ate them. I tried them out on other people, too—Beth, a few relatives over the Christmas holidays, on a friend who had dropped by the store, and even two strangers. A peeled banana on a little round stick, dipped again and again, then frozen. "Hey, that's good. What do you call it?"

"The Chocobonono."

"Hey, that's good. That's real good."

Nothing great is complicated, and the Chocobonono is simple. I merely combine two great things, the all natural and nourishing—yet inexpensive—banana with the universal flavor of all that is holy—chocolate.

I envision them mass produced. Bananas by the thousands trucked in, pulled from bunches one by one, stripped, then jabbed on sticks, moved by conveyor, inverted, hung, hundreds coming down the line, and plop, plunk, glub, glub, as they were dipped in chocolate, plop, plunk, glub, glub again, then conveyed to the freezer, hmmmmm. Later, frozen, wrapped and boxed, then trucked across the country to the markets, trucks with the logo on their sides, Chocobononos By Chris.

I tried to interest Keith in the project. "Hey," I say. "I heard one of our competitors is doing some new desserts. Interburger ought to have some new desserts, don't you think? What about this, a banana dipped in chocolate, frozen, on a stick? Sounds good, don't you think?"

"A what?" Keith says.

"A frozen banana dipped in chocolate."

"What's a bear have to do with a banana?" he asked. "Maybe if we were a monkey company, okay."

"What does a bear have to do with French fries?" I asked. "What does a bear have to do with hamburgers?"

Keith has no imagination. He has to be fired. He is an impediment to the future of us all. The boss must die. If Keith is being fired, everything changes. Chris blossoms, I think. Chris comes out of the cooler. Chris shows what he can do. With something like this, showing initiative, and Wackhoff there, and Keith out on his butt, I will be manager.

"Fried bananas are good," Sammy says.

I peel the bananas, impale them on the little sticks, and lay them on a tray in the freezer. At the proper moment, when the chocolate is hot and the banana frozen, I will dip them once, let them cool, dip them again, let them cool, then dip them all a final time. A triple-dipped, quick frozen, healthy banana delight. The Chocobonono, courtesy of Chris, and patented by him. I will wait and demonstrate this delicacy to Wackhoff. I will sell the idea to Interburger. We should expect this from managers—creativity, initiative, enthusiasm.

"I love fried bananas," Sammy says.

"Just you wait," I say. 'This is food of the gods." I open the can of chocolate and put it on the corner of the grill where it will warm up.

"Cold bananas?" Sammy says.

"Frozen," I say. "A frozen quick-dipped, chocolate-covered banana on a stick. A delightful, new, and nutritious dessert treat. Listen up, Sammy," I say. "Listen carefully." I say the word, one careful syllable at a time, running the last two syllables together more quickly than the rest. "Cho–co–bo–nono." I smile. Then I say it twice much more naturally, as if it has already been born. "Chocobonono."

"What's that?" Sammy asks.

"When the gods on Mt. Olympus ask for ambrosia, this is what they get."

"Ambrosia?"

"Mead," I say. "Neck-tar," said in two syllables with the accent on the last.

"Mead?' Sammy says.

"The Chocobonono."

-8-

Outside I walk around picking up papers and cups, the remains of hamburgers in foil wrap. People are pigs. I like getting outside some of the day. And I want to see Keith and Wackhoff when they emerge from the Lucky Plate. A glance should tell me everything, what they have talked about, Keith's fate. I want to talk to Wackhoff right after Keith is fired, tell him about the grease, be ready for him to tell me the store is mine. Maybe I will tell him about the bonono then. Or maybe that should wait. The bananas are not yet frozen. There will be time.

Then at last I see the two of them come out of the Lucky Plate. I have a plastic garbage bag in one hand, in the other an empty Coke can which has been flattened. I wave. I am sure they see me, but neither waves back.

Strange, they look all buddy-buddy. A gully separates the Lucky Plate and Interburger, and to get from one to the other one has to walk to the highway and then back up the drive. I cannot hear him talking, but Wackhoff never stops, waving one arm as he does to make his point, keeping the other on Keith's shoulder as if to guide him along the right path. Or to keep him, I think, from racing away. Is he fired, or not, I wonder.

Wackhoff's neat attire, the careful cut of his clothes, makes him look like the tent preachers who pitched their tents in an empty lot along Main Street in the Kansas town where I grew up. Inside the tent are folding chairs, benches, a stage of some sort, and the preacher paces back and forth, the Good Book in his hands, thumping it, reading it, waving it about, and always talking. The believers come and sit up front, swaying with the direction of the preacher's pacing, back and forth, back and forth, stretching up their arms, waving, swooning. Folks from town slowly drive by in their cars, stopping for a moment to watch the spectacle. A few are drawn in every night, and the next night a few more, almost hypnotized, getting out of their cars, sitting on the benches in the back, drawn in closer and closer, over time, to the Lord, hallelujah. The preacher never stops, back and forth, back and forth. Someone close stands and whirls and falls. Then another. Ones in the back peer around, and are drawn closer. Back and forth, waving that book, back and forth. Another stands, whirls, falls, is saved. Another stands, whirls, falls, is saved. The fallen are rising, and those in the back are drawn forward. A few more enter the tent, and there is whirling in groups, and falling and rising and saving almost everywhere, and the preacher man is waving his arms and striding, back and forth, back and forth. Hallelujah.

Wackhoff does not break his step, but pulls his sunglasses from his shirt pocket and puts them on. One hand, his right hand, stays steady on Keith's shoulder. It strikes me odd now that he is so engrossed in talking to someone he has fired, but Wackhoff is intense in all he does. He is always smooth, unattached, intense. Keith must be terribly uncomfortable, trapped, forced to listen, leashed by Wackhoff's hand on his shoulder, lashed by his tongue.

The only trash left to pick up are tiny things, cigarette butts, aluminum tabs from soda cans, but I want to be outside, want to see this evolve. It will be, I think, like a storm blowing up, as they do in the Midwest, thunderheads from the distance sending out blades of thin yellow clouds that slice across the sky all of a sudden.

Wackhoff keeps his hand on Keith's shoulder. He will walk Keith to his van, stop him, turn him around, demand his keys. "You're out of here, Keith Schlogger. You are fired." He will pronounce each word carefully. "You're out of here, Keith Schlogger. You are fired." I will be close enough to hear it, but not so close to intrude. I will not gloat. I promise myself that. Not there. Not then. I will save my gloating for when I am alone.

"But I got stuff inside," Keith will say.

"Then you and I, Keith," Wackhoff will say. "We'll set a time when you come back and get what's yours and nothing else."

There will be a firm tone in Wackhoff's voice. I will stiffen, too, on hearing that. Managers should be stiff. I will see Keith's face, the tone in his body, all shift when he realizes that all those years he has given to this place, old unit #38, High Hawk Road, are gone. He will be finished. He will not have me to piss on anymore. And his reward will be simply this, a brief moment on the hot asphalt, a simple demand for his keys, an escort to his ugly van, and me watching him drive away, goodbye.

"I don't want to see you in the store," Wackhoff will say, as if Keith is too stupid to understand what is going on. I will smile, feel good inside, at hearing that. "I don't want to see you hanging around. I don't want to hear about any more stolen grease. Never again. You've done enough." I will pretend not to hear, but continue, picking up the trash that blows about the lot, going about my business of running an Interburger, doing manager's things.

"But who is going to run the place?" Keith will ask. He will be pleading. "The store needs a manager."

"We have a manager," Wackhoff will say. Then he will turn to me. "Chris is our manager now. Chris can do it."

My heart will fly. At last I will be certain. I will rush over to Wackhoff and shake his hand. It will be the perfect moment. Keith will stand there and watch while Wackhoff grabs my hand. Now I will be in charge. Now I will have the keys.

Keith will be silent, speechless, his head hanging. At last Mr. Bigmouth, Mr. Know-it-all, Mr. Put-the-Broom-in-its-Proper-Place, will get his. And I will have been there to see it and relish it. Keith will look at me and smile faintly, as if to say, "I'm innocent," and I have this way of snorting ever so lightly from my nose and rolling my eyes away as if to say how ridiculous he is. Or, maybe he will say, "I'm sorry." I will see that and I will look at him and my expression will not change. Not a whit. I will be unforgiving. I will not be cruel. I will have opened the back door to the store, then I will turn around and look back and Keith will see me then and say "I'm sorry." I will not say the things to him I want to say. Not then. But I will be stone, strong and firm, like Wackhoff. I will look at Wackhoff, and catch his eye, and nod, as if to say, "All things here are under control, no problem," because this will be my store now, and I will be in control.

Keith will get into his van, that ugly purple van with the paintings on the sides, those stupid deer with their horns as silhouettes against the sun, and round windows on each side that bulged out like the eyes of a bug. The door will close. He will start his van. He will look down. He will see Wackhoff standing there, and behind him I will still be in the doorway. Keith might wave. He might break that much, and wave, to Wackhoff who will ignore it, and perhaps he will wave to me. We will be equals now in his eyes. I will ignore that as well. I will be stone. We are equals no more. We are equals only for that brief second when he passes me as he plunges to earth and I am rising. He will hand me the keys, then fall into the burning sulphur. I am not afraid he will think I had anything to do with his firing. He will know better. But he will know, by the way I stand there, at the back door of my store, seeing him crushed like some fat fly, humiliated, stripped of rank and driven off, he will know that I am gloating.

The driveway from the store runs down to High Hawk Road. They are coming up—Keith and Wackhoff—after their long lunch at the Lucky Spoon, and for the moment all I see is their heads above the curve in the drive, the heads in the wavy heat that flutters up from the asphalt. Wackhoff has his arm on Keith's shoulder, like some rope tether to keep Keith from wandering. He is turned towards Keith and talking to him, his other hand in front of them waving up and down, like he is swimming the sidestroke to the shore, rescuing Keith who has swam out too far, who has been drowning....

Wackhoff's hand on Keith shoulder, I know what it means. Keith must not escape. Wackhoff is holding him there like an insect pinned and mounted on display. 'Take this, and this, and this," is what Wackhoff must be saying. 'And another thing....'

I can almost hear them. His arm seems to lead Keith into the shadow of the store. I am still outside with the trash bag in my hand. I prepare to act surprised. Wackhoff turns and motions me in. "You, too, Chris," he is about to say. "You have an interest in this. And I want a witness."

Wackhoff does not let Keith vary his course. His hand on Keith's shoulder keeps him on the straight and narrow, into the office. "Shut the door, Chris," Wackhoff will say. Then he pushes Keith down, forcing him to sit across the desk. There on the desk Wackhoff opens his small black case. Inside are wires and dials and meters. "The game is up, Keith," Wackhoff says. "You know what we must do. A thief in little things, even grease, is soon a thief in the bigger things as well."

He knows about the grease. Wackhoff knows everything. Wackhoff wires him to the machine, wraps a wire around his wrist, a belt across his chest, sticks something to his forehead.

Does Keith know this is a sham, or is it? Or does it make any difference. To be asked the question is to be the liar. Wackhoff moves the needle, traces the lie, by pressing on a button with his knee.

"People don't like you, Keith," Wackhoff is saying. "We gave you High Hawk Road, and you ran it into the ground. We gave you good people, Keith, and you wasted them. We gave you Chris, and you have not listened. You fool around with them in your petty way and waste them. That broom business was bad business, Keith. Bad for the people who work for you. Bad for the unit. Bad for Burger Bear."

Keith looks up. He sees me smile. He looks again, closer this time. Is he smiling, he asks himself. I am inscrutable. Wackhoff cannot see me. Wackhoff is quizzing Keith.

"Do you masturbate? Do you wet your bed? Have you stolen anything from the store?" Wackhoff clicks his tongue. "Have you conspired with others to steal the grease from behind Interburgers? How many times have you been unfair to Chris?" Click of the tongue again.

Keith is sweating. He equivocates on this answer and that. He tries to explain. The needle goes back and forth wildly. He looks at me. He is trapped, and desperate. I mouth the words, but do not say them, slow and careful, so Keith will understand them, "Fuck you."

"You're fired," Wackhoff says. He is emphatic. "You are fired! You are a thief. Now how are you planning to pay us back what you have stolen?" Wackhoff is leaning forward on the desk, supported by his two arms which rest on all eight knuckles and both thumbs. Wackhoff is wearing dark glasses. Keith is reflected of those convex lenses, as well as the whole of this office, and me.

It does not last long. I do not say anything. I have facts, I know the truth, and I do not say a word. Wackhoff is brilliant. Keith signs the confession before him, resigns, agrees to repay the store for what he has stolen, and we agree no charges will be brought against him. We remain inside the back door, in the cool shadow of the late summer afternoon, Wackhoff and I, until we see that van pull away. That ugly purple van pulls out of the back lot and Keith is extruded from my life forever, like so much plastic, so much pasta being squeezed out the end of tube.

Wackhoff turns to me and says, "Okay, buddy. Now, where were we?"

"The store," I say. "We were talking about what was best for the store. And I have a few ideas."

-9-

Their heads and then their shoulders, too, rise up from the curve of the driveway. They seem to float above the surface, buoyed in the summer heat. They come nearer. Wackhoff is talking, his hand on Keith's shoulder. I cannot hear what they are saying.

"What are you doing out here?" Keith asks when he sees me.

"Out here?" I ask, surprised. What does he care? I wonder. Is he even still employed?

I look at Wackhoff, but Wackhoff is standing off to one side, his back to me, talking on his cell phone.

"Who's watching the store?" Keith asks. "If you're out here doing what any ding dong can do, who's inside managing the store?"

"I am managing," I say. "I am managing the store."

"How the hell can you manage the store from the parking lot?" he says. He is shaking his head and growling under his breath. He heads for the back door. Meanwhile Wackhoff gets in his little red Saab, starts it up and without a word to me, without even a look my way, drives off. The top is down on the convertible, and he is still talking on the phone.

The door has closed behind Keith. There is nothing for me to do, but to follow him in.

"What's doing?" I ask. "How was lunch?" I am swimming in a bottomless pool. There is no ground to touch, nothing to stand on. What has happened? I have been dreaming.

Keith goes directly to his desk and is looking over the day's sales figures I have compiled. I follow him into his office, stopping to lean against the jamb.

"You learn anything new, anything interesting?" I ask.

"What's Sammy doing here?" Keith says, without looking up from the figures.

"He's on the back line," I say. "When he finished his Burger Bear thing, he put his clothes back on and starting doing his regular job."

Sammy hears everything being said, but he does not look up from the grill.

Keith looks up and stares straight into my eyes. It is when he stops doing anything else that he is serious. "You were supposed to do the grill. You were supposed to clean up that mess. Sammy did Baptist's job today, and a damned good job he did. You are supposed to be doing Sammy's job. You don't have so many customers you can't handle them."

I don't say anything. I do not know what there is to say. I have anticipated none of this. Keith does not take his eyes off mine. I do not budge for what seems like a long time. Keith is a thief. Surely that is known. But apparently not. Things seem to be as they have always been, the way I hate, the way they have been forever.

I sigh. "I guess I can."

It isn't an issue of cleaning things up. Sammy has done that. He has cleaned the grill and wiped down the back line, the stainless steel, the floor. He has restocked the food for the evening rush, cleaned the fryers, washed the filters, changed the grease. There is little left for anyone to do. But that isn't the point. It is Keith, and his attitude, his pushing, those are the points.

"I guess," he says, but he does not take his eyes off me. I leave. I hate myself. I should stare him down.

"And tell Sammy I want to see him."

I want to tell Keith. I want to tell Wackhoff. I want to talk about grease, and see what Keith says about that. See how he gets out of that. But this isn't the time. I turn to Sammy, wave him into the office with a dip of my head, tie an apron around my waist, put on my hat, push it to one side—to give me that jaunty look men who run the grill must have—then take the spat from Sammy.

"Keith wants to see you," I say, motioning again with a sideways nod of my head.

Sammy has dark, sad eyes. They are steady, so I cannot imagine what is going on behind them. I wonder in what language he does his thinking—French, or Arabic, or Lebanese—or if his soul has lost its tongue and he translates everything into English.

Night Crew

-|-

"I'm off to the bank," Keith says. He is carrying the deposit bag. "Is everything under control here?"

"I got a crew coming in. Shellaine is here," I say. In moments the night crew is due to arrive. There are no customers in the lobby. I have been waiting to ask to Keith about his lunch. What happened? If he isn't fired, what is the score?

"Did you and Wackhoff have a good discussion?" I ask again. Keith has called in his deposit to the home office. Now he has his jacket on, turns out his desk light, locks the safe, and is on the verge of leaving.

"It was fine," Keith says. His face is blank indifference. He will drive the money to the bank and thus end his work day. Nothing has happened; nothing has changed. It is as if I have been dreaming.

"I heard there were changes in the wind."

He looks at me. "What do you hear?"

"Oh, nothing," I say. He makes me feel transparent.

"You must know something to ask such a question," he says.

I feel like a child.

"Like Sammy," I say. "I was wondering about Sammy. Is he going to be Burger Bear full time? Are we losing our grillman?"

I try to sound proud, like 'Wouldn't it be good if Burger Bear had been born in our little store on High Hawk Road on a cold Christmas eve two thousand years ago....' But Keith says nothing. Yet this is the way things ought to be, standing about after a day's work, between shifts, talking about the store, about the people who work for us, about what we knew, about what Wackhoff has told him.

"I mean, is there anything I should worry about, anything I should be doing?"

Keith says nothing.

"I assume everything is fine, you know," I say.

Crazy, I think, that I have to justify my interest in the store I manage every night.

"I assume Wackhoff thinks things are fine here?"

I say it as a question. Something for Keith to grab onto. Something to start something.

"We didn't talk about Sammy," Keith says. "When you need to know something I'll tell you."

I let out a breath in a sort of laugh. It is a nervous habit. "Beth seems to think something is going on."

"Beth?" Keith asks.

"Beth at Southport Mall," I say.

"Beth talks too much," he says. "She thinks she knows too much and she talks too much."

Oh, Jesus, I think. Now I have gotten Beth into trouble. "I bet Wackhoff liked our busy lunch," I say, changing the subject.

"Like it?" Keith asks. He holds the door open. Outside it is still a hot summer afternoon.

"I worried at first when he took over the grill," I say. "I mean, I hate to see a supervisor doing Sammy's work. But he seems to get into it." I wait for a response. "I was wondering if he said anything. If that was okay. If he thought things were going well at the unit, at High Hawk Road. You know."

"He didn't call it a good time," Keith says. "No one wants to come into a store in the middle of lunch and find things so fucked up that he feels he has to get in and run the grill. You know?" Keith waits for an answer, but, he does not expect one. There is no answer to his question. I stand waiting. "He worked his ass off. Thank god he came. We were going down the tubes. No one is better on the grill than Wackhoff, but—no, not a good time. It's my ass when he finds things fucked up here." He looks at me and waits.

"And when my ass is chewed, it's your ass that's going to be hanging over the grease pot."

There is nothing to say. I am scratching my head, and now I put back on my paper hat, tilting my hat to one side jauntily. It is a habit.

"You have your crew under control?" Keith asks.

"I think so. Shellaine's out front. Two other girls come in half a hour. Bryan is coming to do the grill. And Sorenson, of course."

"Why is Sorenson coming in? Why do you have two grill men?"

"I scheduled him in from five to six. Then he comes back at eleven to close."

"Tonight?"

"Tonight."

"I thought we got rid of him. We talked and I said I didn't want him here any more. You said he was a fuck up."

"Well, yeah," I say. "He is a fuck up. You said he was a fuck up and I agree. I agreed to get rid of him. We said that," I say. "But you said not to fire him. You said we don't fire anybody, remember?" I pause, but Keith neither agrees nor disagrees. The sun is about to drop behind a bank of clouds, and there is a red tinge to the late afternoon. "So we decided to make Sorenson's life miserable, so he would quit. You suggested that, so we would not have to fire him."

Keith edges past me and out the door, shaking his head. He wants an answer, not an explanation. And he expects the answer he already knows.

"He hasn't quit yet," I say. Tonight he comes in for a hour, and then back in for closing. It's a shit schedule. I'm on his ass, Keith. But he won't quit. You know what he does?"

I follow Keith outside. I have learned well from Keith. Sorenson can do nothing right. I constantly remind Sorenson of that. He does not flip burgers the way they should be flipped. He does not flip them on time. He is too late in putting down the buns. Or too early. Or they should be neatly in rows. Sorenson always does something wrong. And I can see it and tell him.

And you should center the cheese on the patty, not off to one side. Christ. And you put too much salt on it. God damn it, Sorenson! And how the hell are you going to get the salt off? Shit. No, don't throw the meat away, for god's sake. No, no, no, that's not enough salt now. Oh, god, now you put on way too much. Jesus Christ, don't you hear what I say? Are you too fucking stupid, Sorenson, to fry a hamburger? Are you too fucking stupid to even have a salt shaker? Are you the worst fuck-up I have ever seen in an Interburger hat?

And your grill, look at that mess. Clean up this grill, and mop that floor. You got grease on the floor and someone will get killed. And if you leave it wet, someone will get killed. You are the sloppiest fucking grillman I have ever had to work with, Sorenson, the dumbest fucking trainee I have ever tried to train. How can you have worked here so long and still be such a fuck up? And that's a shitty job of mopping, mop again. And be careful or someone will get hurt. Look at the scum you left on the tiles. Does your mother clean her house like this? And wipe down the stainless. Use a clean rag, for god's sake. And don't use a clean rag all the time, for god's sake. It costs money to clean up after you. But don't push the grease around back here. And wipe your hands, don't touch your hair. People eat what you make, for god's sake. Are you trying to make them sick? Are you trying to make me sick?

And look at that, look at that counter, there's a fry you missed, and a pickle on the floor, and wipe off the ketchup gun when you're finished. Keep things clean. There's always something to do. Wipe down the stainless. Do it again. You missed a spot. And why do you always have to do things twice? And why do I have to always tell you what to do? And carry out the grease, and don't be slow this time, and don't slop grease on the driveway like you did the last time. Don't stay out there and watch the rats. And you're late all the time, and you're wrong all the time, and if you can't do it right then you should quit, Jesus Christ.

So is the message, even if Sorenson never quite gets it. Even if he never acts on it like I intend he should. It is a hard lesson to communicate. It is taking time to train him to do the one last thing for me—to quit. Sorenson needs the money. He needs the job. But ultimately he will quit. I will keep on him. I will show Keith I can do it just as good as he can.

Sometimes Sorenson stays a few moments after he clocks out, comes into my office and sits, his head hanging, almost defeated. "I don't know, Mr. Mann," he says. "I don't know if I can do this." I do not reply. This is difficult. "Do you think I can do this?" he asks. I do not want to talk. I want him to quit, to get mad and walk out. He needs to see the point himself. It will not do if I tell him.

"That's up to you," but I give him time to say he is resigning. I have my answer for him ready. I will agree with him, I will say, "It's too bad, but you tried, but no, it's not working out, and, yes, sometimes it is better to quit."

But he doesn't. He sits in that chair, his head hanging down, maybe waiting for me to say something. His shoulders sometimes shake silently. I think perhaps he cries. Then he reaches up, takes off his paper hat and puts it where he will find it when he comes back another day.

"I'll see you Tuesday," he says on his way out. My heart falls, for Tuesday I will have to go through all this again. He rides out from behind the store on his bike and rings the bell on his handlebar, as if he is exorcising the demons of the workplace. On weekends he comes back for his second hour of work, ringing his bell again. But the demons are always here and waiting.

"He does try to improve," I say to Keith. We stand next to the sunset which is reflecting off the sunset painted on the side of his van. Sorenson is not a bad worker. He is as good as any kid and better than most. He just does not belong here. Who does?

Keith says nothing. He wants Sorenson to quit, and I will make it happen. He opens the door to his van. The door creaks. He steps high to get in.

"I don't want him here," Keith says. "Your payroll is outrageous."

"I ride his ass," I say. "No matter what he does. He cries. But then he works on whatever he has fucked up and he tries to do better. I mean, if I wasn't on his ass all the time, he's pretty good at what he does. He could be pretty good. We might need someone to replace Sammy, and if Bryan goes to days, Sorenson can do nights."

Keith pulls himself up and sits in the driver's seat, rolled and pleated leather. "So," he says at last. "One fuck up can't fire another one. You and Sorenson, a pair."

Keith thinks I don't have it in me, but I do. I will push until I find that point at which Sorenson will not be able to take it anymore, that point at which Sorenson realizes no improvement will ever be enough, that he has no choice but to quit.

"So, what do you want from me?" I ask.

"I want you to do your job," Keith says. He fumbles for the key, inserts it, slams the door shut. I back away. He rolls his window down. "Your labor costs are too high. You're killing us," he says. "Cut back on the hours. Get rid of Sorenson."

He slowly backs out, but stops and rolls down the window again. "By the way, who the hell put the bananas in my freezer?"

It is only rhetorical. I don't think he expects an answer.

"Get rid of them," he says. "Honest to god, Chris, get control. Get a handle on your crew. You got bananas in the freezer and monkeys working for you. Every night it's a circus here."

"A circus?"

"A freak show. And you're a clown. You talk to your friends, you think you are hot shit night manager, should manage this store. But all you do is run a freak show. I've tried, Chris. I'm telling you. I've tried to teach you what I know, but you are a fuck up and always will be."

He looks at me as his window rolls up automatically. He disappears behind the dark and shiny glass. Reflecting in the window pane, the sun rises and sets as he pulls away.

-2-

Bryan's brown grillman's shirt is too small. It fits tight around his shoulders and stops inches above his waist so a ring of flesh shows above his belt whenever he reaches out with his arms.

"You ought to wear a hair net around your belly," I say.

Bryan laughs a slow, deep laugh, no matter how many times he has heard me say the same thing. He is scraping the grill, getting ready to cook.

"You want a banana?" I ask.

Bryan looks at me in his tall goofy way. He often bites his lower lip. He is a senior in high school. His hair is long—more because he lets it grow wild as proof he is a rebel. His hair hangs down over the nape of his neck in the back and over his forehead in the front so, even when he has his hat on, as he does now, he is constantly brushing it out of his eyes. He wears his paper hat cocked to one side. It looks stupid and out of place. When Bryan smiles, he smiles too broadly. He looks idiotic. He especially smiles at Shellaine and everything she says. He is in love.

"It's frozen," he says, looking closely at the banana I hold up in front of him. He takes it and knocks it against the stainless counter. The chocolate coating shatters.

"Do you want it or not?" Bryan is aggravating. He does what I ask, but he never asks questions. If I tell him how to do something, he makes the motions, whether he understands or not. If it is something complicated, he waits me out, then asks Shellaine to tell him what to do. I never know until after the job is done whether he has done it right or not. Bryan does not care. He wants to get finished. From the beginning the point of work for him is to get finished and to spend as much time as he can flirting with Shellaine.

"Frozen won't hurt you. It was dipped in chocolate," I say. "That makes it good."

"That sounds awful," Bryan says. He brushes his hair back and leans over the grill. He is scraping it down to a shine, getting ready to cook for the evening. Soon he will put up a build for dinner—a sixteen and ten, meat, then buns. I could tell him to lay a four and a two hundred, and he lays a sixteen and a ten because that's what he always does.

Traffic on High Hawk Road is picking up. Commuters come in, men grab a quick bite on their way home for supper.

"Looks weird, too," Bryan says, nodding towards the banana. He smiles his big broad smile, then looks at me, then looks back at the banana, so I know he is thinking of some sex joke.

"What do you know about it?" I ask. The banana is frozen solid. I leave only teeth marks in it when I bite. "What do you know about weird?"

Bryan is sixteen. The cuffs of the pants ride high on his ankles, showing his socks and, over the tops of his socks, his pale hairless ankles.

Shellaine is hanging around the back line. She stands where the back line bends around to the front, the same place Keith stands when he watches both sides of the store.

"How come you weren't home today?" Bryan asks her. "I came over to pick you up."

"I worked lunch," Shellaine says proudly. A double is a long day, an accomplishment. She edges her way between Bryan and the hamburgers he is cooking on the grill. In another moment Shellaine has his spatula in her hand. Bryan leans back against the cooler, and listens while Shellaine tells how she and Sammy have done the Burger Bear routine. "Why don't you work the front line tonight, Bryan?" she asks. "I'll cook."

Bryan smiles and pulls his paper hat down to his eyebrows. "I'll work back here with you," he says. He brushes his hair out of his eyes. "If Mr. Mann don't mind."

"You do what Mr. Mann asks?"

"I'll do whatever you ask," he says. There is love, or at least doting in Bryan's eyes.

"We're going to clean the back line tonight," I say. "Sorenson in coming in."

"Oh, man," Bryan says. The crew does not like Sorenson. Sorenson works hard and tries to please, but something about him grates against the others. I figure Sorenson acts too good, is too nice, and his family lives in too rich a part of town for this crew. The other kids hates that. And to them it is not cool to try as hard as Sorenson tries, not cool to be as willing and eager as Sorenson is. It is better to slouch through the night shift, doing only what you have to do, to get by, without seeming to make all that much effort. It is cool to flip a hamburger and toss it to one side, as if you didn't care, but then to see it land exactly where it is supposed to land. It is cool to dress the sandwiches as if you didn't care, but then to have them come out as if you cared a lot. It is cool to act drunk when you haven't yet had a beer, and to act sober when you are so drunk it is difficult to stand. Sorenson is not cool in any of those ways.

"Haven't you fired him yet?" Bryan says. "Man, I thought he was history. Make him work on the front line, Mr. Mann. Me and Shellaine can work the grill together." He smiles at her, and pulls down his paper hat again, and brushes the hair from his eyes.

"Yeah," Shellaine chips in. "You want me to talk to him? I'll fire him."

"You fire him?"

"Could."

She can, too, I think, and quicker than I. At that moment Sorenson comes in through the back door. He is a mid-sized kid, big shoulders, a ruddy complexion and a thick crop of wavy, very red hair.

"Hi," he says, and he smiles. Sorenson isn't an athlete. He is into theater at school. He wants to act on stage or in the movies. He doesn't use his wages to go to rock concerts or to buy beer. He saves his money for college and to go to musicals. He does not belong here. I have to fire him. He should be an usher in a movie theater. He should be working concessions in the lobby.

"You're late," I say.

"I am?" He looks at his watch, then at the schedule hanging by the back door. Sorenson was wearing an expensive watch.

When I first hired Sorenson, I liked him. He was eager for the job, anxious to do things right. But he is almost too meticulous. After he wipes down the counter, he folds the rags neatly and puts them away. When he finishes cooking, he stands back and flicks the crumbs off his apron, adjusts his hat to make sure he looks good, and washes his hands. He is always washing his hands. He keeps a comb in his back pocket and after he washes his hands he combs back his thick red hair.

"I'm not late, am I?" Sorenson asks.

"Just clock in and get to work," I say, shaking my head. No, he is not really late, but I have to begin. Would he never quit? Maybe tonight I can get him to do so.

Sorenson has one bad habit. When he gets nervous, he gets excited, and the more excited he gets, the more nervous he becomes. Often enough in the middle of a rush, when I have been on his case and the other kids have razzed him, he devolves into a hysterical mess. That especially happens when Keith is around. Sorenson must hate Keith as much as I do. Keith could break him, make him quit. So can I, but it will take me longer to push Sorenson over the edge.

"Yeah," he says. "Sure. Sure, Mr. Mann," he says. He is eager from the moment he comes in. He is too damned eager. Bryan is a little slow, a little goofy, but that works okay. Sorenson's bright penny smile grates on my soul. He is grateful for the job. Whenever I regret making Sorenson quit, I see him all smiles, that red wavy hair combed back, pants pressed with a crease, and it makes me mad that he has not quit already. Mad enough to try all the harder.

"Okay, Mr. Mann," Sorenson says. "I'm clocked in. What do I do?"

Sorenson has no regular duties. I schedule him for an hour during the dinner rush, then for an hour four hours later at closing, not because we need him, but because such a schedule should make him quit. 'That's your schedule,' I tell him. 'Take it or leave it.'

Sorenson asks for better hours every time he works. He wants more hours and he wants them together in a row—it is dark at night and he rides his bike back and forth to work—but he takes whatever hours I give him. For the last three weeks he has worked no more than a dozen hours altogether. I don't know why he bothers.

"This place is a fucking mess," I say. "We leave it in a mess and Keith chews my ass. One of you assholes left a broom out last night. So I chew your asses out. And that's the way it's got to be until we get our shit together. Now, tonight," I say, "we're going to clean in and back and around our grill." I nod towards the big grill where Bryan is frying burgers. It has never moved, although it is on wheels. No one has ever cleaned under it or behind it. I'm not even sure it is possible to clean behind it. But tonight Sorenson is going to try. It seems like appropriate work for someone who should quit.

It is hot down there and hard to get to. Sorenson will have to pull the grill out, get down on his hands and knees and climb in and around the shelves and counters just beneath the gas burners. He will do it while the store is open, so he will be in the way of the grillman. I do not know how Sorenson will do it, how he will keep his pants ceased and spotless, his black shiny shoes without a scuff, how long that smile will remain on his face, or what the heat and grease will do to that red wave of hair. It smells of old grease and moldy fries and rat turds back there. Me, I thought, I'd quit if I was told to do it.

"Okay," Sorenson says. "Okay." He is not enthusiastic, but he prepares himself. "But do you think, Mr. Mann, that later, maybe, you might want me to cook?" he asks. "Do you think I can get some time doing the grill?"

"Oh, Sorenson," I say. "You got your job cut out for tonight. Leave the grilling to the grillman for now."

I am probably smiling. I feel like I am going to laugh. Not that the moment is funny, but I feel a laugh. Not crazy. Not funny. But laughter from some deep divide in my heart. The source of oddity. And laughter might keep my heart from breaking.

-3-

When he understands a joke, Bryan laughs. He is laughing now, and he sounds goofy. Bryan has an even temperament. He goes along with most everyone and most everything at work, because he loves his paycheck. It pays for his Firebird, which he loves above all else, except, of course, Shellaine. Bryan is a good grillman for a night grillman. He works hard to pay for his car. He is not fast, nor neat, nor full of grace. He is not even very clean, or quick. He cannot do two things at the same time. He plods along at the simplest tasks. But I like Bryan. He works every night and arrives almost on time. He is dependable. Every month there is a payment due on his car. I know I can count on him until he pays off his car. His infatuation with Shellaine is no secret. Each one of them sometimes talks to me about the other. Bryan tells me how he wants Shellaine to go out with him, how he wants more than just bringing her to work and taking her home. She is fun, he thinks, and funny, and he likes to drink beer with her after work, and talk with the other grill men at the Box-a-Burger while Shellaine is at his side.

Shellaine keeps her distance. She needs the ride to and from work, and she likes hanging out with Bryan at the Box-a-Burger, but she does not want any demands from him. He is afraid of her. That's what she doesn't know. Or maybe she knows. Shellaine likes him well enough. She likes him as much as any boy, she says, but she isn't going to make the same mistakes her mother made and waste her life on men at all. Not like her father. Not like Bryan.

"Hey, Mr. Mann," Shellaine says. She is working the grill while Bryan leans back and watches, his hands folded. "You gonna buy us some booze tonight, Mr. Mann, and go over to Box-a-Burger after work?"

"I got you beer last night," I say.

"We need some more. C'mon," she says.

For no good reason last spring I had starting buying beer for the kids at work. They are all underage, but they want to hang out at Box-a-Burger and there all the kids drink or smoke. Buying it for them is a bad idea, but I find I can use buying beer to my advantage. I use it to make them close the store quicker. I have kept using it long after I should have stopped.

It is easy to do. I duck out for a few minutes and drive across the highway to the liquor store. I had gone to the store to buy beer for myself. The stores were closed by the time I got off work, and a beer or two helped me sleep. Then I started sharing it with my crew. That is not too illegal. But soon enough I was buying beer for them and for their own parties, and not for me alone, and then sometimes even for their friends as well.

"Just beer," Shellaine says. She isn't pleading. She is playing the game. She works on the grill. I am trying to write up a few reports. Bryan is idling on the back line. Sorenson is on his hands and knees wiping up grease that had been spilled there decades ago. Two girls work out front, enough for any rush we can expect on a Friday night. It is a light dinner hour. It is always light at High Hawk Road.

"I shouldn't buy you beer," I say. "I should never have started."

"Hey," Shellaine says. She is squirting catsup and mustard on the crowns of buns, assembling sandwiches, then wrapping them. "It's Friday night. I worked hard all day."

"Me, too," I say.

"Me, three," Bryan says, and gives out that awkward laugh.

"So? Party down, Mr. Mann," she says. "Come on over to the Box-a-Burger."

That does sound good, I think. "I shouldn't leave the store," I say. I say no to whatever they ask, but they know if they ask enough I will go for them. The game is to resist, then give in.

"It's okay," Shellaine says. "I'll keep a lid on things." Shellaine is assistant manager on Sunday nights, my night off. It isn't like I will leave the store without a boss.

Bryan throws ice across half the top of the grill. The ice steams and loosens the scum baked on it. Bryan laughs as the ice boils, then steams and the steam is sucked up the ventilators. I don't know why that is funny, but Bryan always laughs.

"Bryan, goddamn it," I say. "It's too early to clean the grill. It's too cold now to cook. How you going to fry hamburgers on that?"

"We'll cook on the other side," he says. He looks at Shellaine who is cooking, and she does not complain. She is not in charge now, but she runs the store.

"What if we have a rush?"

He doesn't say anything, but looks at me full in the face, then smiles. He brushes the hair out of his eyes. His hair is always in his eyes. We won't have a rush. No such miracle is expected and it never happens. "We ain't never had a rush on Friday night, Mr. Mann. No one comes in here at night. Not a lot."

"But, if they did?"

Bryan looks at me and once again brushes away his hair. He has a goofy grin on his face. Perhaps he is indulging me. He takes his cues from Shellaine.

"Well, don't do it any more," I say. "Not until closing. You guys start closing before the shift has even started."

Shellaine cooks. Bryan cleans the grill, leaving a small square of it hot enough to fry some meat and toast a few buns. Shellaine moves back and forth along the grill, cooking, wrapping, doing all the back line work of the dinner hour. She does not look at Bryan, but pushes him out of her way when she is busy. He smiles and lets himself be pushed.

"Well, let's just hope nobody comes in tonight," I say, meaning Keith or the supervisors. It is possible they might come by and check on the store. Keith has never done it, but Wackhoff does. He has not been by in several months, but he is always a threat. Still, I know my job and there is no reason they will come check on me tonight.

Both Bryan and Shellaine are set in their ways, be it in the little things or in the way they do the essential parts of their jobs. Bryan, for instance, uses both hands to put on his hat. His long hair strings out underneath like a girl's and he should wear a hair net, but that is not cool, so he would never do that. When I mention such things, he only smiles at me, and shrugs his shoulders, and waits for Shellaine to tell him what to do.

"You gonna buy us some beer, Mr. Mann, or what?" Shellaine asks. She rests her hand on the handle of the spatula which is balanced on the grill.

I don't say anything, but I know I am going. I will buy them their beer. They are good kids. And I am as much in love with Shellaine as is Bryan. She could ask more of me and I would do it.

-4-

The registers sit on the counters out front. Other counters hold Coke fountains and hot pies and cup dispensers. Between the front line and the back, a window opens up and when we are busy sandwiches come flying down those chutes, propelled out with a flick of the finger from whoever in the back is running the place. A grill abuts the other side and somewhere underneath all that now is Sorenson, and sometimes his foot and a shoe appear from underneath.

"Don't step on him," I say. "Don't trip." I am up front talking with the girls.

"Euthanasia," Shellaine says staring down at the shiny shoe which is attached to a foot that has somehow slipped out from well underneath all that metalwork. "You ought to kill him," she says. "It would be merciful."

"He won't quit," I say. I shrug my shoulders. Bryan is working the window. He bends down and looks out to the front where he can see and follow Shellaine's every move. His hair hangs down in his eyes. Bryan flicks the sandwiches out so hard they speed down the chutes and hit the end of the tray, flip, spin and roll along the counter, unwrapping and falling into their component parts.

"Dammit, Bryan," I say. I reassembles the food, re-wrap the sandwiches and put them on the steam table where they will stay warm for a few moments. In case anyone comes in. But no one comes in. Bryan thinks he is pretty funny.

"You want me to do it?" Shellaine asks.

"Do what?"

"Fire him," she says, nodding down at Sorenson's shoe. "Sign him up to work for me some Sunday night. I'll get rid of him."

"You think? How would you do it? Bryan!" I say, bending down and looking back through the window when another sandwich comes tumbling our and falls apart. "Would you quit fucking around back there?" He has a big chocolate covered frozen banana in his mouth. He is my first fan. He has taken a fancy to the Chocobonono.

"I'd tell him to quit, that he has a zero chance of getting anywhere."

"You think that would do it?"

"You are being cruel," Shellaine says. "You're like a cat who won't kill the mouse, but you won't let it go, either."

"It's not me."

"You say that. But it's you."

Another BurgerRoo comes flying out the window, unrolls, falls out of its box, and falls into pieces. "Bryan! What in god's name are you doing…?"

I walk around the corner. Three little wooden sticks are laying on the counter. Bryan looks at me and smiles and chews in a deliberate, slow rotation of his jaw, then swallows the last piece of frozen banana. I had made three Chocobononos and put them in the freezer. Bryan has found them and eaten them all. The grill is shiny. He has iced it all down and now it is cool, and a few patties of meat lay on it, pale gray and bubbling. They are baking, not frying.

"Mr. Mann?" Sorenson is saying. I barely hear him. He is far under the counters, behind the grill, with a bucket of hot soapy water and a brush. "Mr. Mann? There's a whole mess of dead rats back here."

"Well, don't eat them," I say. "Unless you want to pay for them. Everything under there belongs to the company. And you, Bryan," I say. "Those were my chocolate bananas. I was saving them for Wackhoff. They were for Interburger. They were the future."

Old Bryan thinks that is pretty funny, and he laughs like he does. I am glad I can make Bryan laugh. It makes the long evenings more bearable.

-5-

There are four people in the store. Two are lined up behind the counter. Two others are eating at the tables in the lobby. This is our evening rush. It is Friday evening. Deadly slow, but I have everything under control.

"Just a six pack of coolers," Shellaine says. "Wine coolers. The same as you got for me before. Some beer for Bryan." She is unremitting in asking me to go across the street and buy her some booze for later that night. She is handing me some money from her billfold. She has asked me half a dozen times already and she will continue to ask until I go.

"What are you guys planning?" I ask. "Special big party tonight?"

Sorenson is far under the grill, sandwiched between the front line and back line and in and among the stainless steel counters. I can't see him, but I can hear him. He is asking for someone to hand him some hot soapy water. "And that big brush in the back. Could someone get me that brush?"

Nobody does.

"No more of that hard lemonade like you got last time," Bryan says. "That made me sick."

"That's what you wanted," I say. "You said you wanted hard lemonade. I didn't want to buy it. I ruined my reputation with the guys who work in the liquor store. It makes me sick to think about it."

Bryan is on the grill; Shellaine runs the window. She is short, and she has to stand on tiptoes to see over the steam table and out front. But she wraps and orders up the grill and keeps an eye on the girls out front who are working, too. Ruth's boyfriend has come in to the store, and is standing by the register. She should not be talking to him, but before I can say anything, Shellaine yells out through the steam table window, "Buzz off, Ralph. Ruth's working. Leave her alone."

Shellaine runs a tight ship when she is in charge on Sundays. If I say anything I am certain to start a fight with Ralph, or Ruth. Shellaine gets Ruth back to work, and Ralph wanders out of the store.

"Wine coolers," Shellaine says. "That's what I want. And whatever beer Bryan wants."

When I watch her at work, Shellaine seems perfect—a kind of beauty, a desire to work and to get things done that few employees have. She works hard and everything moves smoothly. If we need a grillman, Shellaine cooks. When she is out front, she keeps the other girls at work and honest. How can I worry about leaving the store for a few minutes? I could go home and not much would be different.

In fact, I feel good about the store. I am ready to be manager. I even have a replacement on hand. If Sammy is fired for stealing grease – and I have decided to tell Wackhoff, 'It's not really Sammy's fault, he just does what Keith tells him' – but if he is fired, then I can move Bryan to days and give Sorenson to Shellaine. Sorenson is not a bad kid, after all. He's behind the grill cleaning grease. How many kids would suffer such indignity! I feel guilty for having come up with such a job. 'A test,' I call it. But Sorenson has refused the temptation. He does what he is told.

Keith is gone. He is the same as fired. I know it. I can feel it. And everything is changing. I know everything has been the same for too long. I know about Keith and his scam with the grease. If Keith is not fired yet — and Wackhoff might possibly be unaware of the scam — I still had the goods on him and I will get him fired. Then I will be manager. I only worry about Sammy. It really isn't his fault. But then Sammy is Burger Bear, I remember, and all is working out for the best.

"Well?" Shellaine asks. "I can get Ralph to go. He can get us some beer."

"Ruth's boyfriend?" I ask.

Sorenson has crawled out from behind the counter. His pants are smeared with grease and grime and whatever else has collected in the far corners behind the counters and on the floor too far for normal mops to reach. He carries two dead mice in a dustpan and dumps them in the trash. He has dark smudges on his face. Without a word to anyone Sorenson dutifully fetches the brush and hot water for further work in that little piece of hell behind the grill.

"He's old enough," Shellaine says. "Ruth'd make him do it."

"I suppose he would," I say. "I'm going. Let's wait awhile."

Sorenson re-enters in a narrow opening behind the counters that I have never seen. It is a cave, a narrow space that Sorenson has created by pushing and pulling counters about, pulling out the grill on its small wheels that has not moved in years. It is an entrance big enough for Sorenson's broad shoulders. He sits a bucket of soapy water in front of him and pushes it forward with the brush, which he then follows like some character out of Dante descending into hell. No one says anything to him, but Shellaine and I watch as he disappears.

"Bryan! What are you doing?" I ask.

"Nothing." He is at the far end of the back line by the freezer where we keep our frozen French fries. He is playing with the microwave.

"Nothing?" I say. I know he is fooling around, doing something he shouldn't. He has that grin he always gets when he wants to be discovered in his mischief. "You are doing something. What are you doing over there?"

"Nothing," he says again, long and slow, like he is waiting for me to find it out.

"Why are turning on that microwave? What have you got in there?"

Shellaine knows. She is close enough to see. But she stands back and waits for me to discover it. I am the boss. I am in charge. She is just on the clock. She can afford to have fun.

"Want to see something, Mr. Mann?" Bryan says.

Of course I do. It is a stupid question.

"Look at this. " Bryan says. He opens his big hand.

He holds a big black fly in his hand, one of the many that hang around out back all summer. From time to time one finds a way inside where it lumbers around clumsily until it dies, falling into the hot grease, or getting swatted. These sluggish, fat flies are not slow, but Bryan has a knack for catching them, not because he is quick, but because he can move so very slow—oh, Bryan is good at seeming motionless, at work or play— sneaking it up on it until by suddenly closing his hand he traps it. Then the fun begins what to do with the fly he has caught.

"Watch this," he says, and he carefully lets the poor stunned fly loose in the microwave, quickly closes the door, and turns the timer 'On.' "Watch this," he repeats, pointing to get me to look through the window. The microwave buzzes, the light comes on, the little fly darts around inside like flies do, then suddenly erratic in its course as if it has been hit by unseen gusts of air, it pops, and disappears like a tiny firecracker.

"My god," I say. "What the hell are you doing?"

I know exactly what he is doing. I have seen it before. I have done it myself.

"You guys are disgusting. Poor little fucking fly."

"Want to see another one?" Bryan's hand is poised over another fly apparently asleep on the wall.

"God, no, Bryan. Jesus. People eat food that we cook in there, you know."

"A cockroach is better. You want to see a cockroach?" He has a broad smile on his face. To Bryan it is as if he has discovered this, what happens to things inside a microwave.

"No, Bryan, I don't want to see a fly, or a cockroach or any living thing in there. I want to see your ass cleaning this goddamned thing up. People eat stuff we cook in here. I eat it," I say, as if it is the final, and perhaps only important argument. "You make me sick. You are such animals."

He smiles, as does Shellaine. I suppose I do not mean it, and they know it.

"If you two can keep from doing dumb shit for a moment, I will get you your wine coolers."

-6-

Time passes in a burger hut. Like a patty frying on a grill that is set too cool, the evening sits now and the juice of the day escapes. The meat of my life turns gray, more baked and fried and tasteless for not being properly cooked. Under such conditions, the burger is dry and tough and mostly tasteless, but it gets done. And the day is over.

I have a place where I often stand during the evenings, close to the front of the store. There I look out, down across the parking lot and the hump in the hill on which we sit. I watch traffic passing left to right, right to left, on High Hawk Road. It is summer, and the sky remains dark rich red for the longest time, fading overhead from red to blue to black. From inside we are surrounded by a ring of light on the roof from the dancing bears which I have turned on as I do every evening at dusk. Inside I am spared seeing them. I am sick of them. They are old and should be replaced, but Keith likes them and thus they stay. Our other stores, especially the malls, have modern, snappy graphics, bears in natural settings. Ours are vestiges of an Interburger almost forgotten.

I wonder if people in the cars passing along High Hawk Road see me standing here as they drive by, a figure in the window beneath these dancing, rotating bears. They may wonder for a moment why I'm not dancing, too.

"The phone for you," Shellaine says. I can avoid all work when Shellaine is on the clock. Shellaine takes over naturally in a way I do not mind. "Then you better go, you gonna get us our wine coolers," she says.

"Hey, Chris, buddy, what's going on over there?" It is eight o'clock. Night managers everywhere have taken control of their stores, managers have gone home, evening crews are in place, the evening rush in all its various forms is over, and the crew here as everywhere is biding time, serving customers who come in, but mostly waiting to close. "You guys coming over after work?" It is Dandison. I see out the front window the tip of his sign several blocks down High Hawk Road. It blinks like ours but is plain. No stupid bears for Box-a-Burger—a box and a burger that rotate on an enormous well-lit post.

"You," I say. "What are you people doing over there?" I ask. "You got the time to call around and fart off?" I ask.

I am afraid of Dandison. He is me reflected in a cheap mirror. A few years from now, unless something changes, I will be him, doing what he is doing — dying. I hold the same job he used to have, stand in his shoes where he used to stand, and I can only hope I will avoid his fate, ending up in a Box-a-Burger. Odd, because—despite its name—it is a better company than Interburger, Inc. It is owned by a major corporation, and it is growing. A person can follow its stock up and down in the market, and from time to time groups of well-dressed young men with clipboards come by Dandison's unit and advise him on how to improve things. Interburger has none of that. It is owned by a few old men. Our stores are old and dirty. Our methods are antiquated. Burger Bear himself seems like some old Greek myth warmed over and gone stale. We have Wackhoff, and Baptist, and Keith — neither giants, nor gods, nor businessmen really.

I say I have been working all afternoon.

"Another double huh?" he says. "Don't you get sick of it? Keith'll work you as hard as you let him. Always has. Then what?"

"Then what? Things that much better over there?" Dandison has no assistant. He works doubles all the time. His crew is small. He has no Mary Lee to open the store, no Chris to work the night shift, no Shellaine to relieve him on Sundays.

"We're doing great," Dandison says. "I'm doing great. We got a new store going in a few blocks from here. Across the street from you. We're looking for people."

"Great," I say. I am worried. New stores compete for their crews, and a new store close by will compete for mine. He would try to steal them—Shellaine, Bryan, even Sorenson.

"There's benefits to working for a big corporation," Dandison says. "They don't try to kill you by working you to death. At least not as quick."

"Hey what are you so upbeat about?" I ask. Dandison usually grouses as much as I do. "You buy stock in the mother lode or something?"

"I'm not the one working for Keith, friend. Things could be worse than they are, and I would still be grateful I don't work for him."

I say nothing, but I agree. But then I remember I have gossip about Keith.

"And I can go home in a few minutes, if I want to," Dandison continues. That is night manager talk, playing one-up-manship to see who has the shittiest job. "Nobody would mind. My crew can shut this place down. No one from Box-a-Burger is sitting outside, marking my tires, watching my every move. Not like you know who."

"No one is watching me," I say.

"You sure?"

"I'm sure. They got their hands full here," I say. I tell him about Burger Bear and how it looks certain we have lost our day grillman to the marketing department. "He's a good Burger Bear. If Keith is staying on as manager, I hope he loses Sammy. Old Keith, he would have to run the grill until he finds some fool."

"He's got you," Dandison says.

"Don't be so sure," I say.

"You got another job?"

"In a way maybe."

"Oh, man," he says. "That was one reason I called, to see if you and Sammy wanted to work at the new Box-a-Burger. More money. New place. Daytime hours."

"Really," I say. "You'd have a hard time hiring Sammy. He loves Keith's ass. Worships the ground he walks on."

"How about you?"

"Do I worship Keith's ass?"

"You want a job? You looking?"

"Me?" I say, acting surprised, but flattered. "I'm always looking, and I'm never looking." I am being ironic. I see Sorenson's legs sticking out from under the counter. He is on his back and scrubbing. "If you are looking for a night grillman, I have a kid here who needs a job."

"What's wrong with him?"

"Keith doesn't like him."

"Hell, send him down," Dandison says. "That's recommendation enough for me. But we are looking for a new manager. A new store. Day manager. Good money. Thought you might want to talk."

"I don't know."

"It's a good job. Good money. More than you make now."

"That wouldn't be hard to beat."

"And you can dump Keith. Leave him to work a few doubles for a month until he can find another sucker. My super from Chicago will be here Monday. I can get you an interview. Hell, I can get you the job."

Dandison knows the routine. I give Keith two week's notice, or more, and he fires me on the spot. Interburger wants no one on the payroll who is going elsewhere. With no one else to do it, Keith will be working the night shift as well as the day shift until he hires someone new to take my place. I start working for Box-a-Burger right away while Interburger pays me for two more weeks.

"Dumping Keith makes it almost worth it."

"Give me the word. I'll set it up."

"But to be honest," I say, "things have changed. I won't have to worry about Keith much longer."

I warm to my gossip. We have only a few customers out front. From my place in the front window I see them drive up. They park and come in the store, buy Cokes, sometimes a burger, maybe horse around with the counter girls if they are kids which they mostly are. We have a few regular customers, too, but by and large it is quiet, as usual. Next door at the Lucky Plate families come and go. There is a faint riff of music, for it is Friday night, ethnic night at the Lucky Plate, and tonight it sounds Bavarian. Their lot is full and a few cars park in our empty lot. I don't chase them off. A few cars in our lot can only make our store look a bit busier, which is good.

"So?" Dandison says. "What's happening? Nothing as wonderful as Keith getting fired, I don't suppose?"

"That's it," I say. Dandison has hit on it, his hopes converging for a moment with the truth. "I think Keith is getting fired."

"That can't be true," Dandison says "I hate Keith's guts, but Wackhoff and those guys love him. If you are waiting for Wackhoff to fire Keith, hell will freeze over first."

"I don't know," I say, trying to be cagey. "If Keith is fired, and you guys hire him, you will end up working for him. Wouldn't that be the shits?"

"Keith is not going to get fired," Dandison says. "Why would he get fired? They think he is a god over there. Why would they fire a god?"

"Would Box-A-Burger hire him?" That worries me. If Keith is fired, I don't want him around, not anywhere else in the chain, and not as a competitor. "I mean, if he is fired, would you guys hire him?"

"He's not getting fired. That's all."

"You don't think so?"

"Nope."

"Let me ask you a question, Ed. What do you guys at Box-a-Burger do with your grease?"

"Grease?"

"Don't you keep it in a barrel out back, like we do? Then once a month, doesn't someone come by and pick it up and pay you for it?"

"Oh, that," he says. "I don't deal with that. That's corporate stuff, all arranged by the boys in suits. Your managers always sold the grease and kept the money. Here the corporation contracts it out."

"But what if someone was stealing your grease? Stealing from the corporation. What would you think about that?"

"People steal all sorts of shit. All the time. I don't care about the grease. I don't know if someone is stealing it or not. If they do, good luck. That's what I say." Dandison's call has turned out to be uninterested. We have talked longer than normal on the phone. "You know, Chris, Box-a-Burger wants someone right away. I got to act quick. I think it would be worth your time to come talk. The guys in the suits are coming Monday."

"What I'm asking, Ed, is, don't you have people who pay for the grease? Come pick it up and pay you for it?"

"I don't want to talk about grease, Chris. I got customers at the window. You interested in a job or not?"

"But, see, Ed, the thing is that's what Keith's doing. He's got this guy who goes around at night stealing the grease. Your grease."

"I got to go," Dandison says. "I talked you up to the office. I set a time for you, eleven. You need to commit," he says.

"But see, Ed, here's the deal. Keith is stealing, and if he's fired, wouldn't that be great. And High Hawk Road'd be mine. If I get a store, why jump to Box-a-Burger?'

"Hey, man, just think about it, that's all. Come see what they have to say."

"I got other ideas, too. I can turn this place around. I can't tell you everything, but I got this one idea for the menu that I think is hot."

"I got to go."

"Me, too, Ed. But I'd love to tell you about things I would do. There is this frozen banana thing."

"Got to go, Chris."

"Okay," I say, "but the next time we talk, ask me about the banana thing. And I'll tell you how I am going to make a million dollars. And Keith, that stupid Keith, he almost found it out. But he is so anal, all he can think about is picking stuff up, you know? And he was this close to seeing my invention. But all he could see was some bananas out of place." I laugh.

"I really got to go…."

Later working the window it strikes me that my friend at Box-a-Burger has to know about his own grease. A barrel of good grease is worth a hundred bucks or so. I should keep my mouth shut. I promise myself I will from then on. He might tell someone who might tell Keith. Thank god, I think, I have not revealed anything about the Chocobonono.

-7-

The liquor store sits across High Hawk Road. To get there I usually drive a quarter mile down the highway, make a U-turn at the light, then drive a quarter mile back. But this is a perfect summer evening, and the traffic is light, so I walk the distance, darting across traffic that never ceases.

They know me at the liquor store. The man who sits at the register night after night knows all his customers. He watches us, but never says a word. Sometimes, if I buy something silly—sloe gin, or flavored wine, he raises an eyebrow, but he takes my money just the same, makes change and says nothing.

"Guess who came to dinner," Shellaine says when I get back.

I sit the bag in the office and follow her up front.

"Oh, god," I say. Wackhoff is sitting in our lobby with his dinner spread out on the table on his sandwich wrapper—a BurgerRoo, fries, and a shake. He is not eating it, but looking at it closely. He does not look up at me, but he knows I am there.

The rest of the crew is paralyzed. They stand on the back line looking around and watching the supervisor. Bryan is biting his lower lip and brushing his hair out of his eyes. The two counter girls up front are mechanically wiping the counters. When Wackhoff came in, Shellaine says, the crew panicked. It was a surprise. He has come in before, but not for a year, so most of the crew has never seen him. Wackhoff never says much. Like all the supervisors making an inspection, he comes to the store like any other customer, orders a meal, pays for it, and sits in the lobby to eat.

But he sees things. Supervisors see everything. Supervisors see things that no one else sees until a supervisor sees them first—a French fry on the floor that should not be there, an empty napkin holder that until that moment had been full, fingerprints on the glass doors invisible except in certain light. They see these things and anyone can tell when they see something, though they never say a word. They are just another customer. They want food, not cooked for them, nothing special, whatever is on the steam table, and fries, not cooked on the spot, but from among those held ready for the next anonymous customer. A customer might complain about such food, or not. If a customer complains, they might get a fresher meal, or coupons. Wackhoff, like all supervisors, says nothing, but studies the meal he has been given in a bag. He will eventually eat it, and at some appropriate time, when enough time has passed and the supervisor has made his analysis of the store, the manager in charge will appear from the back, will greet the supervisor like, what a pleasant surprise, and, however cold his blood is running, act happy about this unexpected visit.

Wackhoff never looks up, but sits at his table, still in the same light gray suit he has worn since lunch, uncreased from all his day's work. I marshal my crew into action, tell them what it is they should be doing, picking things up, cleaning things up, working, throwing out old food, rebuild the cold and soggy sandwiches that moments before had been ready for sale. "Work, work, work," I say to them. "Never stand around. Do something. Wash the windows." I say it loud enough that, if anyone is listening, I am heard.

I let Wackhoff eat. He sits out in the lobby by himself. We have no other customers. The lobby is brighter in some spots than in others. We turn down the lights after six to save on the electricity. He sits in a dark corner of the lobby, and eats. He looks at his sandwich, to see how it is cooked, to see that it is cooked just so, that there are three pickles as there should be, sixteen pieces of chopped onion or near enough to that, and that the bun is toasted, the sandwich served fresh, or fresh enough. The fries must be crisp. They must be put into the grease quickly, while frozen, and the timer set. Bing! off goes the timer and the fries come up. The grease must be fresh. Only so much salt. Wackhoff has paid for his meal. The change must be exact. The counter girl must give him his receipt and a smile. No amount of fear and trembling must hide that smile.

On the back line we wait. We sweat. Then when it seems he is near done it is my turn, I must waltz out and look about as if I am directing my crew in some task, then, oh, I see Mr. Wackhoff is here. 'Mr. Wackhoff, how good of you to come. I see you have had the BurgerRoo today. I hope it meets your standards.'

Then there is always something. Because this is not just a test. This is not some sort of health inspection to pass, but a training thing as well. 'There is gum on the bottom of this table.' 'There is? Garcon! Garcon! Ha, ha, ha,' I say. 'We'll do the lobby. Thanks for pointing that out.'

But this time, this evening, I was not there when Wackhoff arrived. I do not yet know what Wackhoff has seen. I do not know what he has been given to eat. I am concerned.

"Mr. Wackhoff," I say. "What a pleasure." Then I put on my biggest smile, walk around the front counter, and wipe my hands on my apron—which I have not had on at all, but picked up when I got back from my errand. I take off my paper hat, which I have only had time to put on, not even time to set it jauntily to one side. "I hope you have found everything to your liking."

He does not look up. Instead he picks at the sandwich he has dissected on the table. He has laid out the sandwich wrap and begins to separate the buns, the meat, the pickles again.

"Did you find the secret prize?" I laugh. He doesn't. He acts much like I am acting, pretending he hasn't noticed anything before, just me at that moment.

"I don't like this," he says, looking at the innards of his BurgerRoo spread across the table. "I don't like this at all."

"What's wrong?"

"And who is that fuck back there?" Wackhoff asks. He nods towards the back line.

I turn around and see Sorenson standing around the corner of the front line. His shirt and pants are stained with grease, or with whatever he has found beneath the counters. He is smiling, though, and waiting for me.

"Who?" I ask. "Him?"

"That red-headed fuck. Who is that? Who hired him? Do you have two grill men here at night? Isn't that a lot for a store that doesn't have any customers?"

"Well, he's extra. He's doing some extra work. And you are a customer."

"I've seen him before around here. He's a fuck up, isn't he?"

"Him?" I say. "I guess."

"I thought you were supposed to get rid of him." The pickles are limp and he peels them off the crown of the sandwich.

"I have been trying," I say. "I've given him all this shitty work to do. He's got these hours that no one else would tolerate. He's going to quit. Trust me," I say. "I can be a hard ass."

"Can you?" Wackhoff says, and he looks up at me. He holds a limp pickle between his fingers. "He's still here. He is still on your payroll. Your payroll has been out of control. It's the worst in my district."

"I've talked with Keith...."

"It's not Keith's payroll that is the problem. It's yours."

"I know," I say. But what does he mean, I wonder. Mine? Is this my store now? Is he here playing the bad ass to get me angry, to make me change, to train me? But that is over. Soon enough he will slap me on the back and say, 'By the way, the store is yours.' But then why he is here late at night, pulling apart a burger as if it were a frog in a zoology class? Like all things that have a clear explanation, this seems confused. I don't know how to ask him about this, or that he wants a discussion with me at all. Is he asking, or telling? What rules or reasons govern his thoughts? Is his mind made up or is he seeking? Does my promotion rest still on knowing my answers, or is this some ritual, some initiation to induct me into management, to tear me down before I'm lifted up? If I lie down prone on the floor, if I am nothing, then are we finished with that phase, and then do we begin with my elevation? He knows the answers to the questions he asks. I am certain of that.

"You want me to get rid of him now?" I say, giving Sorenson a quick look, then looking back at Wackhoff.

Wackhoff wheezes and goes back to dissecting his dinner. "No, not now," he says. "Two hours ago. Or two days ago. Two weeks ago. Not now."

I have never understood for sure why Keith does not like Sorenson, but now I suspect it has not been Keith at all, but Wackhoff. And what does Wackhoff know about Sorenson? Nothing. This is not about Sorenson at all. It is the tyranny of grammar. Sorenson is the object of a sentence. 'Get rid of him.' A pronoun at that, and a subject of such force it need only be implied.

Something happened. Perhaps Wackhoff came in some time a few days ago and saw something he thought was weird or out of place. Maybe he does not like red hair. Maybe he thinks there is a lesson here in Sorenson, a lesson to teach, or something to show. Maybe Wackhoff feeds on anguish, and Sorenson is the fruit of some anguish he has sown. Maybe he feeds on power and pain, like others of us feed on BurgerRoos.

"Don't fire him?" I ask.

"Oh, no," Wackhoff says. "We never fire anyone at Interburger. God, you start firing people and the next thing you know we'll be paying double on the unemployment tax. And when people get fired, you have to do it according to certain rules, and you expose yourself to this and that. No, don't fire him now. You don't need to."

"I don't understand."

Wackhoff raises his eyebrows. It's like he is surprised at what I do not know, as if I have never been fired, or have never fired anyone, or have never ridden their asses until they quit, that I do not know how it is done. Or perhaps he is surprised that I do not know it in my bones. Like a manager knows this sort of thing as an instinct. A good potential manager, a night manager, should intuit the truth of this. "You're a big boy. You figure it out."

Or maybe this is humor, and I am on the cusp of being a manager, but I am not yet a manager, and I do not yet know what is funny and what is not, funny being us against them, and I am not one of 'us' yet. But I am going to be. He is waiting for me to show him, and then he will slap me on the back and laugh and say, 'I hope you didn't mind me jerking you around, Mann, but you know that Keith is out of here now, I canned his ass, he's history,' and I will say, 'No problem, no problem, I knew it, I know it, I thought so, but I wasn't sure, he should be out of here, that's for sure, and I agree with you, that's for damned sure.' And he will say, 'It's yours, all yours now, what do you think.' And I will say, 'You won't be disappointed, Mr. Wackhoff, not a bit, I got some ideas, you won't be disappointed, not a bit.' And that's when I will bring out the Chocobonono....

That's what I think. But I sit there for the moment confused. Wackhoff seems weird, but I think it is about to get better, clearer, funnier, the minute I am manager.

-8-

"You left the store," he says.

"I what?"

He repeats what he has just said, then waits for me to respond.

"Just now, you mean?"

He waits without saying a word.

"Well, yeah," I say. "I ran across the street. An errand."

"What are you doing leaving the store?" Wackhoff asks.

"I got some things before the stores across the street closes."

"You drink much?" he asks.

"Oh, no," I say. "It's not for me. I really don't drink that much at all. Not much at all." But then I can't explain to him all that is involved. It is a crime to buy booze for minors, and somewhere surely deep within the manuals it has to be against Interburger policy to buy booze for the night crew. And even if it isn't, it's still a bad idea.

"How much?" Wackhoff asks. "How much is not much at all?"

"Well, not enough to be of concern. Nothing here at work. Never here at all."

"Have you heard about your predecessor Dandison?" Wackhoff asks. I nod. "He drank too much. He quit working at his job, he quit thinking about what he was doing here, and coasted along, and got bored, and when a night manager is bored it is an easy thing to do, to drink a little now and then, then more, then pretty soon you're Dandison, an old drunk who sits back here at night at his desk, and holds his dick with one hand and tugging on this and that without being able to tell the difference."

"I don't drink at work. Not at all."

"It is against the rules to leave the store," Wackhoff says. "You know that. To run across the street, to do an errand, to go buy booze."

He knows. I wonder if he knows who the booze is for. Has he been watching and, if so, for how long. Does he know everything? Can he hear, too?

He has reconstructed the BurgerRoo and is eating it. Did he see the flies explode in the microwave?

"You know the rules. You know you are responsible for whatever happens in this store."

"I know," I say. It is wrong. Clearly wrong. And I have been caught.

"You know that?" He is eating the sandwich. It is obviously cold, and he has picked it apart, laying out the pieces of the BurgerRoo in a patterned arrangement on his napkin. He has tested the pickles, the onions, the meat patty, the buns. It is surely cold now as he eats it, but he is doing more than eating. His jaw rotates slow, like some offset wheel beneath his nose, crushing, mashing, mixing, more than eating, more like inspecting with his tongue, as if absorbing it in his body is a form of understanding, as if in this final union the mysteries are resolved. He sucks in the very energy of life.

"Your grill is set too low," he says.

"It is?" I ask.

"I can tell," he says. "The hamburger is cooked too slow, more baked than fried. And there should be a patina on the meat, a brown sheen, so the juice stays in. The juice is what cooks the meat. It disperses the heat. People think it's blood. It's not. It's juice liberated from the meat and grease. We add the grease at the plant—suet, tallow—to cook just so, to cook just right at the temperature in the manual, and that makes the perfect burger, you know. It is the juice, trapped in this browned meat, sealed in, singed just so, that turns to steam, that cooks the meat and leaves it with its savory taste. The salt, just so and at just the proper moment…." He holds his hands as if he holds a butterfly by the wings, gently and without harming it. He has stopped his chewing for a moment as he beholds his own thought. "It enhances the flavor of it all without robbing it of life. That's what we try to teach you.

That's what we have written in the manual. This," he says, holding out the uneaten half of his BurgerRoo, "is nothing more than old dead meat, cold dead meat, the same as you could buy almost any place, at Box-a-Burger, or even here when Mr. Mann is in charge."

"We should have thrown it away," I say, beginning an explanation, but he brushes aside any explanation I might have.

"Who's your grillman back there?"

"Bryan," I say.

"That goofy asshole?"

I turn around and see Bryan looking through the steam table window, biting his lower lip. He brushes hair out of his face, then pretends to work.

"Well, I guess," I say. "He's okay."

"Or did that fairy cook them?"

"What fairy?" I ask.

"That red-haired fairy that rides the bike. Did he cook this mess?"

"No," I say. "He's being trained. I don't let him on the grill." How does he know that Sorenson rides a bike to work and back? Does he watch this place? How long has he been watching? What does he know?

"Your grillman's been icing down the grill. You shouldn't ice down the grill until after you close. You ice it down, your crew is cutting corners, taking the easy way. Then I have to eat it, you see, your shortcut. That's my job. And it tastes like shit."

"I'm sorry," I say.

"It's baked, not fried."

"Yes."

"And these limp dick fries are not much better."

He holds one up and it is limp, a sorry thing to see. We should have changed the grease that afternoon.

-9-

We sit for a while, and Wackhoff tells me nothing of what I had expected. He eats his fries one at a time, finishes his sandwich, then turns to his vanilla shake to see how much it has separated in a half hour. There is a layer of liquid and a layer of foam on top of it. The froth has separated from the body.

"What about Keith?" I ask when I can refrain no longer.

"Keith?" Wackhoff volunteers nothing, but waits for me to rephrase my question. He takes the lid off the shake cup, stirs the mix, draws some out through a straw. He tastes it experimentally, sips the liquid, holds it up and swirls it around, as if he can tell vast amounts of things from these simple tests.

"Yeah," I say. "I know you talked to him today. I assume you know about the grease."

"I don't know anything about grease," Wackhoff says without taking his eyes off the cup. Held up to the light he can measure the amount of separation. "You have your shake machine set wrong," he says. "It's about ten degrees too cold. You beat this stuff to death if it's too cold. It has the consistency of, I'd say, bird shit. Yes," he says in confirmation, and he nods his head, "Fresh pigeon shit, to be exact, on a winter afternoon."

"The grease out back," I say. "Hasn't it been missing recently?" I say. I try my best to be cryptic. I will give him the facts and let him deduce his own conclusions. From this, he will own it, it will be his as well as mine, and I will be less the tattletale. "Haven't we been earning less from the grease man who is supposed to come by at night and take our barrels? Do you know who has been doing it instead, who has been stealing from us? Don't you know?"

He looks at me, as if for the first time that night, straight on and full in the face. He is expressionless. I have been apprehensive, waiting, begging. Does he not know? Does he not see what this means?

"What do you know about all that?"

I start slow. I wait for him to get it, to put it altogether and see that the manager of High Hawk Road has been stealing from the company for months, for years perhaps, stealing grease and selling it. Keith has not been stealing just from this store, but from many stores, from other Interburger stores, and dealing with the competition.

I start out like this. "Well, you know, or I have heard leastwise, that the grease guy comes by and complains because he is supposed to pick up the grease and he pays us for it, and he comes in and says, I've heard him, there's no grease to be had, and I've heard him say the same occurs from time to time all over."

I get no reaction from Wackhoff for all that. He sucks hard on the straw, sucks in his cheeks, and draws down the shake by a third. The froth remains. The liquid is gone.

I move closer to the point. "So what I have found out is this, that Sammy, you know the day grillman Keith has here, the Burger Bear today, you know, that Keith has him go out at night, they bought a truck, the two of them, at night with some other Lebanese that lives with him, that lives with Sammy, and they go out into the night, like one o'clock or later and hit the grease barrels, I mean I guess they do what the grease man does which is pick up a barrel, leave a barrel, but they don't pay, they steal the stuff for all I know, and anyway so Sammy says it's Keith who sets this up, who tells him where to go and when, the whole thing's fixed, and even if he is kicking back to managers or so, that's stealing, and even if it is okay, I mean, managers are not supposed to do this sort of thing, work like that, it's not an Interburger thing, it's a conflict, and all, you know," and my voice and thoughts dribble out like a wave hitting on a beach. I have washed up as far as I can go, then I must pause, as I am sucked back into the ocean. I sit and watch Wackhoff's face. The tide is going out.

Wackhoff has finished his shake. He makes a gurgling sound with the end of his straw as he sucks up the last of it. He sits his cup down and belches, not disgusting like, not offensively, but low and slow, as if it is a final test of flavor and quality. His eyes remain on me, impassive as before, but he says nothing.

I feel a little desperate. "I assume you know," I say, "I'm not a rat. I thought you were taking him to task for it, this afternoon up there where I could see you in the Lucky Plate, and firing him, and then, well, that leaves a problem here, I mean old Sammy's not at fault and a good grillman for sure, but who's to manage this place then, if Keith is canned, and then the problem of a night manager, you need a crew, and there are plenty of things that could be changed, that's for sure, with Keith gone, the lid's off my idea of a frozen chocolate covered banana which I have named the Chocobonono, but then again this might not be the time nor place for discussing that."

Wackhoff is tidy, as always. He puts his trash back in his paper bag, even folding up his napkin he has used, but which he has not used at all. He hasn't needed it.

"It is sort of like a business," he says to me at last. "Not an Interburger thing, but then not everything is Interburger, now is it?"

"No," I say. "But....."

"It's an arrangement I have with Keith," he says. "This grease thing. In our spare time. I wouldn't say we steal the grease. It's more. We arrange for it."

"I see," I say.

"What's grease?" he says. "To us, we throw away what we can't feed to our customers. But out there," he continues. "Someone out there uses it for cleansing cream. Do you know that?"

I know that, I told Sammy that very thing that afternoon. "But what about Keith?"

"Keith," he says, "is leaving High Hawk Road. You are right on that. But they are making him a super. He is going to have a dozen stores from now on. All the new stores we open west of here are his."

I close my eyes. Too much is going on. Keith is leaving High Hawk Road. But he remains a danger. He may not be here to find another broom misplaced the night before, but he will be here to find something. I am not free. Keith is a thief. But so is his boss. There is more, but I cannot hear it. I open my eyes. Nothing has changed. Wackhoff is still there.

"It's almost closing. I should check on my crew," I say.

"Your crew?" Wackhoff says. "What if I told you someone else is now night manager of this store."

"Like who?" I ask.

"Like Shellaine."

"You mean you might make her night manager?"

"Would she be good?"

"She would be great," I say. Wackhoff does know this store. It is, I think, as if he has read my mind. "She would be my choice."

"That's good," Wackhoff says. "She is my choice, too."

"Let's tell her," I say. "When does she start?"

"Half an hour ago," he says. He is looking steadily at me. I cannot tell from his calm presence what he is looking for in my face, but he is looking for something. "I told her while you were at the liquor store. While you were where you were not supposed to be. While your crew was serving me this crap for supper."

-10-

I do not want to ask another question, but I need to know. Or maybe I want to ask the question, but I do not want to hear the answer.

My crew is closing the store. Shellaine stands where the night manager should stand, between the front line and the back, directing both, making sure the crew moves on now, cleaning what can be cleaned before the door is locked.

"If you are looking for your friend Sorenson," Wackhoff says, "he's not here."

I am not looking for Sorenson until Wackhoff mentions his name, but then I look and I do not see him.

"She fired him. I saw him leave."

"I didn't think we fired people here," I say.

"Well, I assume she made him see the way things were. How long's a person going to stay where there is no hope?"

Something is terribly wrong. Shellaine has the stuff to do this job. But where am I in all this? I should have hired her. She should know she is mine—to promote and to fire.

Someone comes in the back door. It is Beth. My face flushes red. "Oh, my," I say. "Do you know Beth? She works at the Mall...."

"I think she is terrific," Wackhoff says. "The best we have."

"She's good," I say. I don't want her to be in trouble. We should not have fooled around together. It is against the company policies. 'Dipping your pen in company ink,' is how Keith would describe what is forbidden.

"Maybe she's come to see Shellaine," I say.

"Maybe."

"So," I say. "What about the job?" I ask. "Keith's job? Who's the manager going to be? Do I get it?"

"You?" Wackhoff says. "Not you."

"No?"

"No."

"What happens to me?"

"You're fired."

I cannot move. I cannot think. The chairs in the lobby are bolted to the floor. They sit up against little tables that are bolted to the floor as well. The chairs swivel, but not much. Enough so I feel I am losing my balance, falling forward, falling forever. I hold on to the edges of the table, one hand on each side to steady me. I do not want to reveal anything to him. I feel no pain. I am stone.

"I didn't think we fired people here," I say. "I didn't think that was our policy."

I surprise myself. I should be pleased. I am free. I hate this place. I hate this man in front of me. I have wasted all this time. And yet I sit here still wanting this job, angry that I do not have it. Worse, I want to be promoted and that has escaped me, too.

Worse, worse, I am fired. In a company that has a policy not to fire anyone, I have been fired.

I look back at my crew. They are working, but they were very quiet. They know. Everyone knows. Shellaine must know, and she must have prepared them. Now Beth must know. I am the very last to know. I am dead.

"In your case, we've made an exception," Wackhoff says. "We don't fire people willy nilly. Like your little friend Sorenson. If you fire people like that because you don't like their faces, it will raise your unemployment rates, and that can be sky high in a place like this. And it is bad form. Guys like your friend Sorenson, hell, they can be our best customers. You don't want to piss off a customer. So, with guys like that, people like that, counter girls, you know, that type, we like to have an agreement that it is in the best interest of the worker to go elsewhere. You know? And sad little guys like Sorenson are bread and butters to lawyers out here in suburbia. Under age. Fired without cause. The little poof. Discrimination. How many have fathers or uncles that are lawyers and would sue us? But in your case I don't expect that. I don't expect you to know where your best interest is any more. If you knew that, what have you been doing here for two years? You who have been without hope. You haven't been able to figure it out yet. Why would you figure it out now? In cases like you, we fire your ass for cause. If anybody questions us, we tell them you left the store while you were on duty and went to buy liquor for minors."

-11-

Short of giving him my keys and asking him how I get my final check, there is no reason to stay longer. I keep nothing personal in the store, no magazines, or papers, no address book, no booze. The last thing in the store that was mine had been the three Chocobononos that Bryan ate. At least my secret recipe is safe.

So I leave. I would have driven away without saying goodbye to anyone, even Beth, but I am gripping Galinda's steering wheel so tight I cannot let go, not even enough to take out my keys and start my car. I sit there a while by myself, hearing the traffic on High Hawk Road until I am certain that time has resumed.

I relax enough to put in the key and turn on my radio. I have said it often, this radio has been worth the price of the car. The speakers have a richness to them, and they give the empty hulk of my old Galaxy the semblence of an auditorium. There is space enough inside for music to turn and weave. Some thirty miles away a university radio station plays jazz at night. Early in the evening the jazz is complicated, and thoughtful, and aggressive. It makes my mind buzz when I listen to it. It makes me think. But as the evening wears on, say after two hours, it changes, becoming mellow, a single musician kind of jazz or a duet, or trio, soft and mostly in a single line that weaves in and out, a reward for hanging on. Later still, if anyone is listening, as I often am, the mellowness turns odd, the lines of song twist about in strange ways, like a drunken bumblebee in love. It resonates with madness. We are not there yet, but I have loosened my grip on the steering wheel and feeling has returned to my hands.

Wackhoff leaves. He does not look my way. He exits from the front of the store and never looks to the back where I sit in the dark in my old car. He walks down the front drive towards High Hawk Road, then later I see him walking up to the Lucky Plate. His car is parked there, and it is situated so he can sit in it and see everything that goes on in the store. He has been there all evening. He has known everything and always has.

Galinda starts and dies.

-12-

At first I do not know whose bicycle it is. But then I know it has to be Sorenson.

"Is that you, Sorenson? Are you out there sneaking around? I hear your bell. Is that your bicycle?"

He comes out of the shadows walking his bicycle. He has been ringing the bell so I will not be scared as he approaches.

"Did I scare you, Mr. Mann?" he asks. "I didn't mean to. I'm sorry."

"You come back to kill me or something?"

"Oh, no...."

"Cause if you did I wouldn't blame you. But you're too late. I'm already dead, my friend. Interburger's done me in. There's not much left to me, but a pile of regrets and this car that won't start."

Sorenson looks at poor Galinda and in the dark it seems to care more for the death of my machine than for me. "I'm sorry, Mr. Mann. I'm returning my uniform. Ms. Beth said that I am terminated, but it wasn't final until I brought back my uniform."

"You are too good, Sorenson. You ought to keep it as a souvenir. What are they going to do, raid your house to get a grillman's shirt and a paper hat or two? I doubt it."

"I just want my check."

"But I'm glad you're here, Sorenson. I'm glad I have a chance to tell you I'm sorry for all the shit I put you through. Climbing under that grill, giving you hours that no one should've had to work, riding your ass all the time. I don't know who that was. It wasn't me. What was I thinking?" There are a dozen bears on the roof of the store and they run around on a little track, lights flickering. Their arms go up and down mechanically. I have worked here so long I associate each of them with people who work at Interburger—Keith, Wackhoff, Sammy, Mary Lee, me. I have been a part of that mechanical parade. "I wanted that job, that management thing," I say. "I got the bug. I wanted to be the boss. Imagine that — me, a boss."

"You weren't so bad...."

"I hate the boss. And I'm sorry that I started to act like one."

"There's always a boss. You don't want to be the one who carries out the grease, do you?"

"I don't know." I'm not talking to Sorenson. I am leaning against my car and looking up at the night. Here in the shadows from behind the store the sky seemed much darker, stars brighter, and the noise from the street below is muffled. "I don't want to care about the grease. If it is any consolation," I continue. "I only lasted ten minutes more than you. I'm fired, too, Sorenson. Ten minutes. That's what a college degree and five years of experience will get you."

"I'm sorry you lost your job," Sorenson says. He has lowered his kickstand and is folding his grillman's shirt nicely. "At least you don't have to come back and turn in your uniform."

"No. But it wasn't much of a job."

"You should be doing something more than working in a restaurant," he says.

"Really? What do you suggest? One job seems to me about the same as the next, and they're all pretty much frying hamburgers and getting rid of grease. Teaching school, vice-president of marketing, repairing bicycles, playing football, brain surgeon, digging graves—all pretty much just flipping one kind of hamburger or another. Tossing on two pickles and giving a squirt of ketchup. That's pretty much it. I don't mean to sour you on work."

"Oh, I don't mind the work," Sorenson says. His voice is light, buoyed by some irrepressible force. He is happy and I do not understand him. "I liked it well enough that I got me another job doing pretty much the same. Head fry cook nights at Box-a-Burger. I start tomorrow. Mr. Dandison says someday I'll get my own store."

I laugh. Dandison has been successful in hiring someone. "Good," I say. "Maybe someday I'll work for you."

"Okay," Sorenson says without irony or sarcasm. "Then you can clean out the dirty rat turds behind my grill." He laughs, and he deserves to laugh. And maybe someday I will work for Sorenson. I have nothing better lined up.

"Maybe so," I say. "Gotta work somewhere."

"Anyway, come down to Box-a-Burger. Mr. Dandison says everybody comes down after work and has a beer or something. Box-a-Burger uniforms are really pretty cool. I'm getting a new grillman's shirt and a hat tonight. They are black and orange, and you can wear tennis shoes."

-13-

I am there, in Galinda, in the dark, in front of the wheel, when the boys come to pick up their girl friends after work. Sitting in front of the store, the lights to their cars off — there were two of them, each in his own car — their cars idle, low rumbles coming from below, and their tape decks play a mindless mix of rock. Soon enough the lights go out in the lobby. The girls come out, one at a time, kiss their boyfriends, jump in and those cars rumble off to some other Friday night that is young in beginning.

I sit in Galinda, both my hands gripping the steering wheel, staring straight ahead, when the last three come out. They have been talking, and they act surprised to see me.

"You going down to Box-a-Burger, Mr. Mann?" Shellaine asks. Bryan is carrying the sack of wine coolers. He stands behind her a few steps. He is smiling that fixed broad smile that on anyone else would be a smirk.

"I might," I say. I only turn my head. My hands are fixed to the wheel. They grip so tight, it feels as if they will never let go.

"Then we might see you." I have never seen her do so before, but when she turns she touches Bryan on the elbow. That gentle little touch turns him all around and sweeps him to his car. Things are changing that I do not understand. Could they possible be in love? Beth is left standing as they drive off.

"Waiting to kill someone?" she asks. "You angry?"

"No, not angry," I say. "I don't know what, but not angry. My car died."

"Oh," she says.

I look ahead, through the windshield. She leans against the car. I can feel her warmth in the cool evening breeze. I can smell her scent of fresh talc.

"Poor Galinda."

"Poor Galinda," I concur. It takes a few minutes for me to begin to relax, but I do. I ease my grip on the steering wheel. My hands are numb.

"I tried to tell you, you know."

I crack open the door and turn, my feet hanging out. The dome light comes on. We have spent many evenings like this, spring and now summer, with her, or with the crew from High Hawk Road at the Box-a-Burger.

"You tried to tell me what?" I ask.

"Wackhoff came to the mall store today. He had talked with Keith, and Keith had his promotion. He told me about it, then offered me Keith's job."

"I see," I say. "They made you manager."

She nods. She is tall and thin. She has the longest neck of anyone I have ever known. Her breasts are small. I have seen men with bigger breasts. But the thinness of her arms and legs, the crane-like length of her neck, a fragility of her features, her length, as if she were a straw that could be blown about with almost any wind, there would be no mistaking her for a man. All this I have always thought of as lovely. I still think that.

"Why not?"

"I don't begrudge you getting it," I say. I stammer a bit. "I wish I could celebrate more…."

"I asked Wackhoff, what about you? But, they had made up their minds, these guys, and they don't want a lot of what about this and that. He asked if I wanted it and I said yes. That's the way that has to be. They want an answer."

I wait for her to continue.

"I didn't know they were going to fire you," she says. "I wasn't sure."

"I should've known."

"Are you really that unhappy?" she asks. "Did you want the job?"

"No," I said. "Yes." I smile. "I stayed too long. So long, a part of me wanted to be the boss. An unnatural desire. I should have gotten fired a long time ago. I should have made them fire me on my terms. I have two weeks free with pay. Free to do what I want. No one to tell me what to do, how to do it. How often do any of us have that?"

"Don't you think I will be a good manager?"

"You'll be great. It's just…."

"Somebody's got to be the boss," she says.

"You think?"

I fancy I see a look of fear or disappointment on her face. Her hair is short, and auburn, and it seems so fine it moves, however slightly, with the slightest puff of air, turn of her head, my breathing. Last night there were no bosses and no slaves, but all at once. No one to watch at the window, no one to carry out the grease. It was exceptional, singular.

"If there's an Interburger," I say to break the silence, "and we must have the dancing bears, then, yes, I agree, there has to be a boss. Otherwise," I say, "I'm not so sure."

-14-

The fender rattles as the truck pulls in behind the store. It is dark. The headlights are off as if they were concerned about disturbing the universe. The truck carries a dozen barrels.

"Looks like someone wants to make some cleansing cream," I say.

The truck stops by the grease barrels and a large, hairy monster gets out. His head and paws are enormous. But the monster wears a paper hat printed with a picture of Burger Bear.

"Good Christ, Sammy. What are you doing?" I say. "You can't go around in the middle of the night dressed up like a bear!"

The bear stands back, then dances, first on one foot, then on the other, then back again. "Burger Bear, Burger Bear, who are you? Burger Bear, Burger Bear, Burger—Roo!"

Behind him his brother on the truck wrestles a full grease barrel around and rolls an empty one off to leave in its place.

"You are insane, Sammy," I say.

"I am going to dance for the kids tomorrow."

Sammy backs up a step or two, returns his hands to his hips, and in a moment is dancing from leg to leg, his hands above his shoulders. "Burger Bear, Burger Bear, what to do? Burger Bear, Burger Bear, we love you-u-u-u-u-u-u-u." He turns and he dances away, hopping and singing. He dances into the cab of his truck, and after grinding the transmission, pulls away, his friends holding onto the barrels of grease which bounce and slosh as they drive away.

-15-

I have no idea what I am going to do, not that night, not tomorrow, or tomorrow night. The rest of the weekend. The rest of the week. The rest of the year. Forever more. No idea. I turned to the jazz station. And I listened to jazz. The later it gets, the better the reception is.

"Let's go home," I say.

"What is home?"

"Is that a 'yes' or a 'no'?" I ask. We are standing, I think, but I am not sure. Beth is close to me, wrapped under my arm. Or we may have been sitting on the edge of my car seat, the door open, she sitting on my one leg propped up, close to me, wrapped under my arm. Or on the hood of my car, lying back, looking up at the stars, close to me, wrapped under my arm. Maybe all of these things.

"There's the job at Box-a-Burger, if you want it."

"Oh, yeah," I say. "Box-a-Burger. I should've taken the job when it would have given Dandison some pleasure to think he was stealing me from Keith. Now it would be more like picking up Keith's trash."

"It's not bad," she says. "Maybe you can get your own store. They open stores all the time. They are opening across the highway."

"I heard."

"Dandison could get you hired."

"You think?" Yesterday I had hoped for something more, for getting above this business altogether, inventing new foods. Now that seems like a distant dream. It all seems like a dream. Her breath goes down my chest. Her head is tucked under my neck and fits perfectly. Her hair brushes against my cheek as if she is lashing me with her gentlest thoughts.

"You want to go down there," I say, "and have a beer or something. I'll drive."

"Okay," she says. "Okay." At first she sounds tentative, but she warms to the idea. "I guess it would be okay, this one more time yet. You know, since I am hardly the new boss to hang out with the crew. Sure," she says.

Galinda surprises even me. She starts right up this time, no problems, no hesitation, not even smoke from her exhaust. She sounds smooth, like new, like she has been reborn. She is more than a radio that night. I touch the brakes. Even she responds with the grace of new love.

"The new boss's not done yet," I say. "Here's a hint. The bears." I nod my head to one side.

She sees me nodding at the store. She turns and looks.

"You have to turn off the bears."

There they are, well lit and turning, dipping, rolling back and forth on little hidden tracks in endless loops. Some call that dancing.

"They're your bears, now," I say. "Me? I'm a banana man. And I'm not done either. I'm going to make that chocolate banana thing work. No Interburger for me. No Box-a-Burger. All that is behind me. I'm into something else. I may be back here in a week or two with a truck full of Mr. Christopher Mann's Bononos. Sell them to the kids. Sell them to you to sell to the kids.

Manufacturing. Distribution. I may have been on the wrong side of things, you know?"

Beth says nothing. She leans her head lightly on my shoulder.

Night air is cool and clean. It is good to inhale deep. "But here," I continue, "you're the boss. You turn on the bears, and at night you are supposed to turn them off. They have to rest."

"You're right," she says. She seems to disappear into the swirl of darkness that envelops the back of the store. I hear her open the door, imagine her disappearing into even deeper darkness as she goes inside, then the bears halt and the lights go off on the roof. The night is unimaginably even darker.

There is freedom in this silence, to move and to rest. To love and be gentle. She is inside swimming through the night; then, she is suddenly incarnate, a presence around which my arm is wrapped.